STAR WARS ®

JEDI QUEST

THE MASTER OF DISGUISE

JEDI QUEST

CHOSEN BY FATE.
DESTINED FOR CONFLICT.

#1 THE WAY OF THE APPRENTICE

#2 THE TRAIL OF THE JEDI

#3 THE DANGEROUS GAMES

#4 THE MASTER OF DISGUISE

SPECIAL HARDCOVER EDITION: PATH TO TRUTH

STAR WARS®

JEDI QUEST

BY JUDE WATSON

THE MASTER OF DISGUISE

LUCAS BOOKS

SCHOLASTIC INC.

New York   Toronto   London   Auckland   Sydney
Mexico City   New Delhi   Hong Kong   Buenos Aires

www.starwars.com
www.starwarskids.com
www.scholastic.com

No part of this work may be reproduced, stored in a retrieval system, or transmitted in any form or by any means, electronic, mechanical, photocopying, recording, or otherwise, without written permission of the publisher. For information regarding permission, write to Scholastic Inc., Attention: Permissions Department, 557 Broadway, New York, NY 10012.

ISBN 0-439-33920-0

Cover art by Alicia Buelow and David Mattingly.

12 11 10 9 8 7 6 5 4 3 2 1   2 3 4 5 6 7/0

Printed in the U.S.A.
First printing, November 2002

Civil war had raged on the planet Haariden for ten years, and even the ground showed the scars. It was pockmarked with deep holes left by laser cannonfire and grenade mortars. Ion mines had blown hip-deep craters into the roads. Along the sides of the pitted road, blackened fields burned down to stubble.

The Jedi had heard the explosions from cannonfire all afternoon, echoing off the bare hills. The battle was twenty kilometers away. The wind tore across the fields and whipped up the dirt on the road. It brought the smell of smoke and burning. The gritty sand and ash settled in the Jedi's hair and clothes. It was cold. A watery sun hid behind clouds stacked in thick, gray layers.

To Anakin Skywalker, it looked like something out of his nightmares. Visions of a world of devastation, where a cold wind numbed his face and fingers, and he trudged endlessly without arriving at his destination. He gave no outward sign of fatigue or discomfort, however. He was training to be a Jedi, and being a Jedi was all about focus. A Jedi did not notice the pelting grit, the razor-edge of the wind. A Jedi did not flinch when a proton torpedo's blast split the air. A Jedi focused on the mission.

But Anakin was not yet a Jedi Knight, merely a Padawan. So though his pace never flagged, his mind kept slipping away to brood on his own discomfort. He was cold and hungry and there was a small pebble in his boot that was driving him crazy. The sky seemed to grow lower and lower, pressing on him. He would be glad when this mission was over and he was back in space again, shooting past bright stars.

He could take the cold and the danger and the empty stomach. But he had grown up on the Outer Rim planet of Tatooine, and he hated the sand. He hated swallowing and tasting it. He hated how it found every opening, every gap in his tunic and leggings. He hated how a stray speck always managed to lodge in his eye.

Ahead of him walked his Master, Obi-Wan Kenobi, with another Jedi Knight, Soara Antana. The two Jedi kept their gazes sweeping the road ahead, alert for the telltale sheen of a life-form sensor half-buried in the dirt — a trigger for an ionite mine. Next to Anakin trudged Darra Thel-Tanis, a fellow Padawan.

He glanced sideways at Darra. Her bright copper and gold hair was dulled with dust. He could no longer tell the color of the bright ribbons she had woven through her slender Padawan braid. Her eyes were on the road ahead. Her pace hadn't lagged since they'd begun this mission. They had been walking for three days. She did not seem to register the fatigue Anakin was feeling.

She must have felt his eyes on her for she leaned closer to mutter under her breath.

"What I would give for a bath."

"And a cold glass of juma juice," Anakin added.

Darra sighed. "Whatever you do, don't say that again."

Anakin would have grinned, but he didn't want to get sand between his teeth.

Ahead Obi-Wan and Soara walked at the same steady pace. The focus of their concentration was complete. Not a stray pebble or slight disturbance in the dirt missed their notice. One wrong step and a mine could blow them into the leaden gray sky. Although Anakin and Darra had received some training in mine-spotting at the Temple, there was nothing as good as experience to alert the unwary to the danger.

The Jedi had been called to Haariden on a mission to rescue five scientists who were on a Senate-sponsored mapping mission. They had been caught on the planet when hostilities suddenly erupted after a cease-fire. The scientists had been pinned down in the country-side. Unable to get to their space cruiser, they had sent an urgent distress signal to the Senate. The two forces on Haariden had agreed three times to a cease-fire in order to give the scientists safe passage, only to erupt into violence again before the scientists could get to their vessel and leave. Finally, the Senate had appealed to the Jedi for help.

It was feared that the scientists would be held as hostages or bargaining chips in the battle. Outsiders had not been welcome on Haariden, and the political climate was volatile. Each side thought the Senate was in league with the other — and thus all visitors were vulnerable to attack. Afraid of being captured, the scientists had moved from deserted village to deserted village, just ahead of the soldiers. The last communication the Jedi had received was three days ago. They could only hope that the scientists were still some-where in the area. Time was running out. Roving patrols posed a constant danger. They had been walking since daybreak, searching one abandoned village after an-other. Some had been almost completely destroyed, others intact but eerily empty of life. The population had moved beyond the mountains and had set up refugee camps there.

"Tenuuri is ahead," Soara said, consulting the map on her datapad. "Let's hope we find them there." She scanned the far distance, her keen gaze analyzing the puffs of smoke from the grenade mortars. "The battle is getting closer."

"It will be dark in an hour," Obi-Wan said. "That will be better for us."

Soara grimaced. "Maybe. Haariden may be low on large-scale weapons, but they have plenty of night-scopes. They fight anywhere, anytime."

Through the wind and dust, Anakin saw shapes ahead. Small buildings, built close to the ground. The village. On one side he saw trees stretching to the hills. The trees looked strange, and with a jolt he realized why. The trees had leaves. All of the trees he had seen since landing on Haariden had been bare, their branches blasted by battles fought weeks or days ago.

"After we find them, we can double back through the forest to the transport," Obi-Wan said. "We'll cut three kilometers off our route."

"At least they left some trees standing," Darra said. "I don't understand how two forces can destroy every-thing beautiful on their home planet and just keep on fighting. What is left to fight for? Have you ever seen anything like this?" she asked, waving at the ruined fields and deserted village ahead.

"Yes," Obi-Wan and Soara said together. They exchanged a glance full of a knowledge Anakin did not understand.

The shadows were long on the road now. They walked into the empty village. Heavy shelling had taken place here. None of the houses or businesses were intact. The wood had burned and the rocks lay in piles, some of them as tall as Obi-Wan.

If the scientists were here, they had hidden well. The Jedi did not want to call out. There was always a danger of snipers in this area — snipers who did not distinguish between visitors and enemies.

They searched methodically through the half-destroyed buildings. Anakin's heart grew heavy as he kicked through the debris of ordinary lives. A pot, battered and black. A boot. A scorched roll of bedding. A toy.

There's not much to a life, when you think about it, Anakin considered. As a boy on Tatooine he had longed for nice things, expensive things, for his mother. Once a space merchant had come through the slave hovels with fabric for sale. He remembered how Shmi's hand had lingered on a rich piece of cloth. He remembered the color, a luxurious ruby. He remembered how it burned inside him that he was unable to buy it for her. How he had vowed that someday he would . . .

I won't think of it. Focus.

Darra stood frozen. She gazed down at a tiny crib. A scorched piece of linen trailed on the floor.

"Darra." Soara's usually brusque voice was soft. "Come along."

They moved through to the next house. It had suffered a direct hit. There was only rubble. Anakin could hear Darra's slow, even breaths beside him. He knew she was concentrating on her breath, slowing it down, trying to focus. Anakin also felt disturbed. It was as though his nightmare went on.

They walked back onto the street and stopped in front of the next building. Obi-Wan and Soara exchanged a glance. Anakin reached out to the Force. It always took him just a beat slower than Obi-Wan to feel it. The Living Force was here.

Obi-Wan headed left, Soara to the right. With a glance, they ordered their Padawans to follow.

Soara went first, headed through the doorway like shimmersilk. She was known for her grace and flowing movements. Obi-Wan followed, keeping to Soara's left. Anakin and Darra stepped through.

The building had once been a café. A long counter

was charred and blackened. Some tables and chairs remained, but most had been splintered and blown apart. A very large round oven sat in the middle of the room, the size of a small landspeeder. It had been vented through the roof by a stone chimney. The chimney lay in ruins around them.

A rusty metal door swung on one hinge on the oven. Soara and Obi-Wan fanned out on either side, motioning to their Padawans to do the same.

Soara bent over and gently moved the oven door.

There was a muffled gasp. A small rustle of movement.

"Don't be afraid," Soara said. "We are Jedi."

"Prove it." The voice was male and wobbled a bit, fear disguised as bravado.

In a movement so fast Anakin could have blinked and missed it, Soara unsheathed her lightsaber, activated it, and held up the glowing beam in front of the open oven door.

"Thank the stars and galaxies," the voice breathed.

A face smeared with ashes poked out from the open door. "Needless to say, it is good to see you. I am Dr. Fort Turan. Space geologist. Head of the mission. Objective is the study of the effects of volcanic activity . . ." A shoulder poked out, and then an arm. ". . . on planetary atmospherics . . . *oof* . . ." Dr. Fort

8

Turan tried to wiggle his ample body through the small space. ". . . within a scale three system." The rest of Dr. Fort Turan popped out. Despite a torn tunic and a nasty scrape on one cheek, he beamed at the Jedi. "Now, meet my team."

A blue-skinned arm poked out, followed by a face. "Joveh D'a Alin, at your service. Degree in tectonics with an emphasis on mineralogy."

Joveh D'a Alin slid out. Another face appeared. It was another human male, this one smiling broadly. His hair was caked with dirt and stuck straight up, and his brown eyes were warm. "Dr. Tic Verdun. Practical theorist, planetary origins. Very glad to make your acquaintance. For a moment we feared we would be roasted alive."

The next scientist to emerge was a Bothan named Reug Yucon, "special training in atmospherics, trans-system and galactic." Then a slender Alderaan female named Talie Heathe, an oceanic specialist.

Dr. Fort Turan rubbed his hands together. "So. Shall we retire to your transport? The sooner we're off this planet the better."

"We can leave right away," Obi-Wan said. "We're about eight kilometers away."

Dr. Fort Turan's face fell. "Eight kilometers? So far?"

"You have speeders?" Reug Yucon asked.

"No," Obi-Wan said. "Speeders would attract too much attention. We have to walk."

"That will take a long time," Joveh D'a Alin said, concerned. "We had hoped . . ."

Tic Verdun looked at his fellow scientists. He tried to appear cheerful. "Not so far. And we have the protection of the Jedi now. It's a fine night for a walk, I'd say."

Talie Heathe picked up on Tic Verdun's attempt to cheer them. "But let the Jedi lead, Tic. You've done enough for us."

"Tic has saved our lives many times over," Fort Turan said. "He's scouted ahead and kept us moving away from the soldiers."

"He did a good job," Obi-Wan said. "You stayed alive. But the battle is close now. We'll be walking in the opposite direction. We should be able to make good time."

"We have provisions for you," Soara said, reaching into her survival pack.

Quickly, the Jedi shared water and protein cubes with the scientists. They looked a little better when they had finished.

A pale pink moon was rising as they left the village and entered the forest. The shelling had stopped, and the area was eerily quiet. The faint hazy light of the moon barely penetrated the thick trees. They did not dare risk a glow rod.

They walked for several hours. Soara kept track of their progress with her datapad map. "We're making good time," she murmured to Obi-Wan. "Another kilometer and we can turn and head south."

Anakin smelled the battle before he sensed it. He breathed in and smelled smoke and fire and death. Ahead, Obi-Wan and Soara had stopped. Darra drew a ragged breath.

The scientists had smelled and sensed nothing. They continued to walk until Obi-Wan held up a hand to stop them.

"Slowly," he murmured.

They walked, making no sound. In a few minutes Anakin could see that the light through the trees ahead had changed slightly. The smell was worse now. The wind brought it to him, and it smelled like something in a dark dream.

"The forest ahead," Soara said. "It's gone. Burned."

"They must have fought closer than we'd thought," Obi-Wan observed.

"Which means there could be patrols nearby."

They exchanged a glance. "We have no choice," Obi-Wan said.

"Padawans, we must surround the scientists," Soara said. "Keep close and alert."

They left the shelter of the trees. Around them were blackened stumps. A laserfight had taken place here. They hurried through the eerie landscape, the pink moon tinting the devastated forest with a rosy light that made everything seem even more dreamlike to Anakin.

There was no longer a path. They stumbled over branches and stumps. They kicked through spent shells. They were losing time. The scientists were exhausted. Their footsteps lagged.

Then Anakin felt what he had hoped not to feel on this long night: the dark side of the Force. It was around them, somewhere in the night. He knew Obi-Wan and Soara felt it, too. It took another minute for Darra to frown and place her hand on her lightsaber hilt.

"What —" she began, but the night suddenly exploded into spasms of light.

Anakin felt the impact of a shell hit him like a wall of air, and he went flying.

CHAPTER TWO

Anakin landed and tasted blood in his mouth. He had bit his tongue. He lay on his back, looking up at the black velvet sky and the pink moon.

"Everyone okay?" Obi-Wan shouted. The blast had knocked them all flat, but Obi-Wan and Soara were already back on their feet.

"Stay low!" Soara directed as the soft *wee-ooosh* of another airborne weapon came toward them.

Anakin cleared his head, jumped to his feet, and ran toward the scientists. He and Obi-Wan herded them toward the shelter of the fallen trees. They took cover as another shell exploded. Dirt fell like rain.

"Not again," Joveh moaned, her head in her hands. She was shaking.

Tic Verdun put a hand on her shoulder. "Just a few bombs. Nothing too scary."

She lifted her head and tried to smile. "Nothing I haven't seen before."

Soara and Darra were quickly taking readings. They hurried to crouch next to Obi-Wan and Anakin.

"They're close," Soara said. "Maybe half a kilometer away. Heading toward us. They must have a long-range bioscanner."

"I'm picking up coded communications," Darra said, pointing to her comm sensor. "Lots of them. It's got to be a large force."

"Who are shooting first and asking questions later," Obi-Wan said, ducking as another blast shook the ground.

"Can you jam communications?" Obi-Wan asked her. "That's a start."

"I can try." Darra bent over her scanner and began pressing keys. In addition to being a superb fighter, she was an expert at communications.

"Half a kilometer," Obi-Wan repeated, thinking.

"And closing," Soara said.

"With this moon, they'll be using nightscopes and goggles."

"I agree," Soara said tersely.

Another explosion flashed. They felt the shock wave

but it had landed clear of the area. The scientists exchanged concerned glances, but no one spoke again. They watched the Jedi, knowing that the only way out was to follow their lead.

"A Padawan–Master team, or should we do it?" Obi-Wan asked Soara.

She thought for a moment. Anakin didn't know what the two Masters were planning, but he knew one thing — he wanted to be in on the action.

"Got it," Darra said suddenly. "They're jammed for now, anyway." She glanced up at them, her expression taut. "They'll override the jam pretty soon."

Soara nodded, then turned to Obi-Wan. "We'll need all of us," she said. "It's too large an area."

"Yes." Obi-Wan turned to the scientists. "You must stay undercover. If we don't return in fifteen minutes, go back the way we came. Hide where you were before."

"You're leaving us?" Fort Turan asked.

"Not for long." Obi-Wan grabbed one of the extra survival packs they had brought on this mission. He motioned for Anakin to take one.

"What will happen to us if you don't come back?" Reug Yucon asked.

"We'll come back," Obi-Wan said.

"If you'll come back, why did you tell us what to do if you don't?" Joveh D'a Alin pointed out.

"Scientists. You're so logical," Obi-Wan said. "I said that for your own reassurance. We will be back. Come, Anakin."

The four Jedi slipped off into the velvet night that was so suddenly and spectacularly lit by flashes of deadly light. Anakin could feel the Force gather around them. He did not often have the experience of feeling the combined Force of two powerful Jedi Knights as well as their Padawans. It made his vision sharper, his senses clearer. He knew where the explosions would come. He heard the faintest of *sss-sooop* noises when the grenade launcher fired. He could tell the direction without even thinking about it.

The Jedi headed straight into the advancing troops. Soara and Obi-Wan explained the plan. In the survival packs were luma grenades, projectiles that released particles of intense light. They would fan out along the advancing line and toss the grenades straight at the troops. Since the troops would be wearing night-vision goggles, the effect of the grenade would be doubled. A majority would be blinded for at least an hour. Plenty of time for the Jedi to lead the scientists to safety.

The difficulty would be to launch enough grenades amid what would no doubt be heavy firepower. The Jedi would have to work fast and keep continually on the move. They would also have to coordinate their efforts so that a wide area was covered.

Obi-Wan and Soara gave their directions in low voices. The Jedi fanned out. Anakin counted off the seconds, then lobbed his first grenade.

The night lit up like a flash from a nova. Anakin kept his eyes away from the light. He hadn't expected so much illumination. Even with his Jedi training, it was hard to see. His eyes adjusted, but he stumbled as he ran. He threw another grenade. Then, taking another leap, he threw a third.

He could see the troops clearly now. The front lines were kneeling, their hands over their eyes. The others were shooting blindly.

He dodged the fire and threw another grenade. He dashed to the rendezvous point, where Obi-Wan and Soara were waiting. Obi-Wan and Soara scanned the field as Darra ran up.

"The right flank," Soara said.

The right flank was the area Anakin had been assigned.

"The lumas hit behind a wall. We need more cover there."

"I have grenades left," Darra said.

"Go."

Darra didn't pause. She ran off, already pulling the timer release on her luma grenades. The sky lit up in a series of flashes.

Anakin watched as Darra twisted, leaped, and rolled as she lobbed several grenades in a precise pattern designed to box in the troops. He saw where his grenades had missed. He had never seen the wall. He had become disoriented.

"Darra has the benefit of seeing the wall from this angle," Obi-Wan said. "It would have been impossible to spot it from your position."

Anakin's face burned. It was kind of his Master to point that out. Still, he felt badly that another Padawan had to return to do his job.

"We're done here. Let's go." Soara spoke and motioned to Darra at the same time. Darra leaped the final few meters and caught up to them as they ran back toward the scientists. The night was dark again, and there were only a few random explosions, hitting the ground far from them.

The scientists were standing, waiting for them. Without a word they joined the group and they hurried through the rest of the blackened forest.

They jogged the first kilometer, then slowed to a fast walk. They had left the site of the battle behind, and the trees rose around them again.

"There's a village ahead," Soara said. "We should skirt it."

Obi-Wan nodded. "We need the cover of the forest for as long as . . ." He stopped.

The two Jedi Masters exchanged a glance. Anakin felt the disturbance in the Force. It seemed to be coming from all around them.

"Down," Obi-Wan said crisply to the scientists.

The Jedi all activated their lightsabers at the same time. They made a circle around the scientists and were ready as the patrol burst out of the trees.

The rebel Haaridens were armed with repeating blaster rifles. Some had wrist rockets. Anakin could see at a glance that the Jedi were outnumbered. And with the scientists to protect, it could get tricky.

The blaster fire was fast and it seemed to be everywhere at once. Anakin did not give another second of thought to the numbers against them. He focused so completely on the battle that everything else fell away but the movement of his lightsaber and his attention to where the blaster fire would strike next.

Smoke rose around them. The leaves began to scorch. Obi-Wan leaped to destroy a rocket headed straight for them. The midair explosion sent air thudding against Anakin's eardrums.

The squad suddenly concentrated a third of their

troops to the left and made a surprise strike close to Darra. Anakin saw it coming before she did. She was only a split second behind him, already turning to deflect the blast of fire. She had to pivot on her left leg, leaving her right side slightly exposed.

"I've got it!" Anakin shouted to her. He leaped forward, his lightsaber moving in a constant arc.

But Darra had already compensated for her move. She had shifted and turned, and the two Padawans collided. Darra was thrown to the side.

Blaster fire ripped into her leg. She gave a cry and fell, and her lightsaber went flying, lost in the confusion of bodies.

"Anakin, cover me!" Obi-Wan roared.

He leaped and scooped up Darra with one arm, keeping his lightsaber moving, deflecting the fire. Anakin jumped in front of them, desperate to help his Master. Soara herded the scientists closer together and, with a heroic effort, charged straight at the troops. Anakin leaped over the scientists to join her.

The fury of their attack caught the troops off guard as blaster fire ricocheted back into their ranks. Their line began to waver. Anakin and Soara pressed the advantage while Obi-Wan and Darra retreated with the scientists.

"They're going to regroup," Soara told Anakin. "Let's go."

They turned and ran after Obi-Wan and the scientists, who were dashing through the trees.

"The village," Obi-Wan said to Soara. "We need cover now."

Darra said nothing. She slumped against Obi-Wan, and he lifted her into his arms. Her eyes closed and her lips parted. Anakin felt a deep shudder go through him. She looked as though her life energy was draining away. And it was his fault.

CHAPTER THREE

Get in and get out. That was the goal of a rescue mission.

It never, in Obi-Wan's experience, worked out that way.

They had angered the Haariden patrol. Obviously the troops knew they were Jedi, but the Haaridens did not care. They were after revenge now.

Obi-Wan carried Darra along the twisting trail. They were close to the village and temporary safety. Every once in a while the patrol pursuing them would set off a rocket. It always fell short of their small band. But it was not a comfortable distance.

Obi-Wan remembered another world, another day. Qui-Gon carrying a desperately weakened Jedi Knight — his close friend Tahl. He remembered how Tahl's hand kept slipping off from around Qui-Gon's neck. *It is too late for me, my friend,* she had told him.

He had seen the refusal to accept the fact in Qui-Gon's eyes. At the time, as a Padawan, Obi-Wan had thought it impossible that a Jedi Knight could die.

Perhaps the first moment of his adulthood was the moment he had seen Qui-Gon's face when he realized that Tahl was dead.

Why am I thinking about death? Obi-Wan wondered.

It was this planet. Ever since he had landed on it he'd felt uneasy. The darkness here was more than a result of cloud cover. It hung in the air. The Force dimmed with it. He knew it had affected his Padawan. Anakin was sensitive to the dark side of the Force. He felt it sooner and deeper than Obi-Wan had at his age.

Darra would be all right. A blaster wound to the leg was serious, but not life-threatening. Yet her limp body and her slip into unconsciousness worried him. There was a disturbance in her Living Force. He could feel it.

"The village is ahead," Soara said. He could see in her face that she, too, was worried about Darra. "They are not giving up."

"We must stop. Darra —"

"Yes. I must treat her."

The village had been large and prosperous. That was easy to see, even in the close darkness. Clouds covered the pale moon as they filed swiftly through the streets, looking for the best shelter they could find.

Soara and Obi-Wan chose a building packed in the middle of a crowded street. Thanks to a half-destroyed wall, they would have lookouts on all four sides. Yet there was enough shelter for Darra to stay warm.

They wrapped her in a thermal cape. Soara administered bacta to her wound.

"It doesn't look bad," Obi-Wan said.

A line appeared between Soara's eyebrows. "That is what worries me," she said in a low tone. "She should not be unconscious."

"Will you allow me?" Joveh D'a Alin spoke up gently. "I trained to be a medic before my scientific degree."

She came closer and bent to examine Darra. She touched her with gentle, expert hands.

"Without instruments it is hard to tell," she said. "It appears that she is in shock. Is it possible that the blaster bolts carried a chemical charge?"

"It is possible," Soara said. "It is what I feared."

Obi-Wan saw his Padawan swallow. Anakin's eyes looked dark in his pale face. Obi-Wan knew that his Padawan felt responsible. Anakin had leaped impulsively, not trusting Darra to evade the fire. As usual, his Padawan had thought that he was faster, stronger, than anyone else.

The problem was that it was often true. But not always.

"She needs care that we cannot give," Joveh D'a Alin said. Her gray eyes were compassionate. "But her vitals are still good. The bacta should help."

"We need to get her to the Temple," Soara said. She reached out and, with one finger, touched the dusty fabric in Darra's braid.

"Master, I will go," Anakin said.

Obi-Wan turned, distracted. "Go where?"

"To the Haaridens. I will negotiate a truce so that we can continue to the transport."

"What makes you think you will get within a hundred meters of a Haariden without being attacked?" Obi-Wan asked.

Anakin kept his gaze steady. "I am prepared to risk it."

Obi-Wan shook his head. "No. That is not the solution."

Soara joined them, closing her comlink. "I've contacted the Temple. They will pressure the Haaridens for a cease-fire. But it will take time. No one is sure who is in charge on either side. They are sending a medic to us, but it will take two days." She glanced at Darra. "What if it's too late? Can we risk moving her? Can we carry her to the transport? It's still kilometers away."

Obi-Wan had never seen Soara look so uncertain. If

his Padawan had been lying so still and pale, he would have felt the same way.

Tic Verdun spoke up. "We can all take turns. We aren't as strong as the Jedi, but we won't let you down."

"Thank you," Soara said quietly.

"We have other options," Obi-Wan said. "I'll be back."

Anakin took a step toward him. "Do you need me, Master?"

"No." Obi-Wan hurried away. He regretted the brusqueness of his answer immediately, but he would work quicker alone. He needed his own perceptions. And, although he didn't like to admit it, he needed time alone to think of a way out of this. When he'd told Soara they had options, he'd meant it. He was sure they existed — he just didn't know what they were. He did not think that carrying Darra over kilometers of rough terrain while being pursued by an attacking force was the best idea.

Obi-Wan shifted from shadow to shadow. He explored the village thoroughly. When he'd finished, he knew that the village had once had three bakeries. He knew who the mayor had been and that she'd had three children. He knew that the schoolteacher had driven a yellow speeder.

He just didn't know what to do next.

He saw a faint light through the forest. He climbed

to a higher vantage point and trained his electrobinocu-
lars toward it.

The patrol was camping outside the village. No
doubt they did not relish a night battle. They would attack at daybreak, he was sure. They knew that the
small band was trapped.

Obi-Wan shook his head. He could hardly believe his
eyes. It seemed such a short time ago that a world
such as Haariden would respect the Jedi, or at least
fear the Senate enough not to attack a rescue mission.
Had the Senate's power eroded this far? Had the galaxy
ceased to respect the Jedi as well?

You don't need speculations. Just answers.

He walked slowly back to the hiding place, hoping
an answer would come to him on the way. He had
hoped to find a small, forgotten cache of weapons.
Some usable transport. But anything that had not been
destroyed had been looted.

Obi-Wan stopped. *Not looted,* he suddenly realized.
The village had not been looted. It did not bear the
scars. It had undergone a siege. That he could tell. But
the valuables hadn't been stolen. They had been *re-
moved.*

He retraced his steps. He combed through the
buildings, now knowing exactly what he was looking for.

It didn't take him long. He found the first tunnel

opening in the closet of a prosperous house that was almost empty of furnishings. The opening was set into the floor of patterned wood panels. If he hadn't been looking for the seam, he would have stepped right over it. It was cleverly concealed in the design on the wood.

He lowered himself down into the tunnel. It had been clumsily dug, but it was reinforced well with plastoid tubing. He kept his bearings as he wandered through the underground walkways. There were several exits. One was in the back of the school. One in the clinic. And one opened out deep in the forest, on the other side of the Haariden camp. They were so close that Obi-Wan could clearly see the weariness in one soldier's face as he leaned over to unroll his bedding on the forest floor.

Obi-Wan returned to the others and beckoned to Soara. He explained what he had found.

"Should we evacuate now?" Soara asked, glancing at Darra. "We'll be taking a great risk if we try to sneak by the Haariden camp."

"Too great a risk, I fear," Obi-Wan said. "If it were just the four of us, it would be one thing. But we can't count on the scientists. They've been on the run for weeks. They're worn out. I think we need to strike an offense first. Now. They are settling down to sleep. It's the best time. If we can knock out their tracking devices and some weaponry, we'll be ahead."

Soara nodded. "You and I must go. We should leave Anakin here in case."

Obi-Wan nodded. He was glad Soara didn't hold Anakin's rash action during the battle against him.

But when he told his Padawan their plan, Anakin seemed crestfallen at not being included in the attack.

Obi-Wan felt exasperated. Anakin's reaction seemed that of a boy, anxious to be in on the action. It wasn't worthy of his Padawan. "This is important," he told him. "You need to protect the scientists and Darra. Soara and I won't be long."

"But you might need me," Anakin said. "It's a large patrol."

"We have surprise on our side. No, Padawan. You must remain here."

"I would not fail you this time," Anakin promised.

Obi-Wan saw it then, the hunger on Anakin's face. It was not a hunger for action. It was the need to redeem himself.

Obi-Wan spoke gently. "The best thing you can do for Darra is remain here to protect her."

Anakin looked down, struggling to accept the order. "As you wish, Master."

"You must keep your focus, young Padawan," Obi-Wan murmured, so that the others wouldn't overhear. "This is not a judgment on you. This is the best way to proceed."

Anakin nodded, keeping his eyes down. "All right," he muttered.

Obi-Wan hesitated. Now he could feel the shame behind Anakin's questions. His Padawan's feelings ran deep. His shame was filling him now, and he thought that only action could relieve it. He was wrong, but Obi-Wan would need time to explain why this was so.

He knew that his Padawan needed him. Yet he had to go. He struggled for words to leave behind, but he had none. The only thing left to do was walk away.

CHAPTER FOUR

Anakin watched his Master walk away from him. There was no doubt or hesitation in how Obi-Wan moved. Ever. Anakin wanted to move through his own life with the same assurance. Yet time and again he found himself confronting miscalculation and error. Time and again he moved when he shouldn't have moved, said what he shouldn't have said, or turned when he should have stayed still.

It was times like this when his connection to the Force felt like a burden more than a gift. It pulsed around him so strongly and he could feel it so easily that he used it to act instead of to strategize. Obi-Wan had told him the Force must be used for caution and control as well as action. So far he had not learned that lesson. It was because he did not understand it. During the battle he had seen which way the blaster fire would come. He had exactly determined its movement and speed. But he had not factored in the notion that Darra would be moving, too.

If it had been a Temple exercise, it wouldn't have mattered. Darra would have perhaps received a bruise at most. She would have landed lightly on her feet, the way she always did, and turned to him with a quick retort and a smile. Instead, she was wounded and in shock.

Nothing had gone right on this planet, Anakin thought, almost angry now. He felt lost in a dark world, spinning in a system he did not know.

The scientists had rolled themselves into thermal blankets and were trying to catch a few hours of sleep in the corner. Through the half-demolished roof above, Anakin could see the cold night sky. The constellations were not familiar to him and made him feel even farther away from home.

He crossed the room and crouched by Darra. Her eyelashes cast shadows on her pale cheeks. There was a fine sheen of perspiration on her skin. He watched her breathe in and out.

I'm sorry, he spoke in his mind.

He felt a presence by his shoulder. The scientist Tic

Verdun looked down at Darra. "It is hard to see a friend this way, I know."

"Yes," Anakin said. He did not want to discuss his feelings with this stranger.

"Yesterday I would have said that Jedi are used to pain and suffering and thus can bear it better than we do," Tic Verdun continued. "Today I find I would be wrong. You seem to feel it more."

"Not more," Anakin said. "It's just that we put ourselves in the way of danger. It is our path. We see one another's strength. We see one another at our best. So we know exactly how much we lose when one of us goes down. And we feel . . . if only we could have been the one to fall."

He felt Tic Verdun's eyes on him. "I saw that you wanted to go with your Master and Soara Antana. If you wish to follow them, I will take responsibility for Darra Thel-Tanis and the rest of us. The others are tired. I am still strong."

Anakin was impressed. No wonder Tic Verdun had been the group's scout. He had great courage.

Anakin shook his head. "I can't go. But thank you." He turned away again and sat down next to Darra. He didn't want to be rude, but he wasn't in the mood to talk.

But Tic Verdun didn't get the hint. He sat down, too. "The Force," he said. "You have to see how it would be intriguing to a scientist. Something that cannot be seen, cannot be measured. And it can only be felt by a select few. Here I am with someone who can feel it and use it. I saw it happen just a short while ago. Can you explain how it works to me? Can you tell me anything at all?" He added hastily, "Or is it forbidden to speak of it?"

"It is not forbidden," Anakin said. "But it is not done."

Tic wrapped his arms around his knees. "I see."

Now Anakin was afraid he'd been rude. "It is hard to talk about it. It is something I can feel around me. Something I can gather and tap into, like a deep well. It sustains me and frustrates me —"

"Frustrates you?" Tic's dark eyes were alive, curious.

Anakin leaned back against the cold stone wall. He felt very tired. "Sometimes. It is so vast . . ."

"That you feel small." Tic gave a sad smile. "I study the galaxy. I know how that feels. How simple it is, and yet how intricate and complex. It is all around you and you are at the center of it, yet you are nothing compared to it."

"Yes," Anakin said. Tic had put into words what he had been feeling. No one had ever done that before. Not even Obi-Wan. Sometimes the Force made him feel . . . lonely.

"And you will never truly understand it," Tic added softly, "yet you will spend your life trying. And sometimes you ask yourself, is it worth it? Is it foolish of you to devote yourself to trying to know the unknowable?" He laughed. "All I know is, it can't be wise."

"Wisdom is not what we seek," Anakin said, repeating a Jedi saying. "Wisdom can only be found."

Tic shook his head, grinning. "Whatever that means. And I thought the scientific institute was hard."

When Tic smiled, Anakin realized that he was younger than he'd thought. He wasn't much older than Obi-Wan. Tic had made him feel better, and he didn't think anyone was capable of that.

Suddenly the sound of explosions split the air. The scientists all jumped to their feet, fear on their faces. Darra stirred but did not wake.

"What is it?" Reug Yucon whispered the words harshly.

Anakin heard the sound of alarmed voices from the Haariden camp. Soara and Obi-Wan had begun their attack. Every muscle seemed to contract with the effort of staying still. He wanted so badly to go.

"Should we leave?" Joveh D'a Alin asked anxiously. "We could be trapped here."

"No," Anakin said. "We'll wait here."

Waiting was the hardest thing. Like him, the scientists wanted to move. But they wanted to run from the source of the explosions. He wanted to run toward them.

"We are lucky to have you with us," Tic said quietly.

A small consolation, Anakin thought. But he'd take it.

CHAPTER FIVE

If any of the Haaridens were trying to grab some sleep, they were now disappointed. The patrol troops had been so certain that they were safe that they hadn't bothered to post guards. It was easy for Obi-Wan and Soara to sneak into the camp. The Haaridens had left the small arms jumbled together in a heap. Soara and Obi-Wan easily jammed the flechette launchers and the missile tube, and pocketed all the thermal detonators.

Then they tossed a detonator into the brush in order to wake everybody up. While the Haaridens scrambled for their blasters, the only weapons left to them, the Jedi stood, waiting.

Before the quickest Haariden could shoot, Obi-Wan called, "Think first. Surrender is your best option."

The Haariden captain spoke up, his blaster leveled

at Obi-Wan's chest. "Why should we surrender? We are forty, and you are only two."

"I can think of one good reason," Obi-Wan said, holding up the thermal detonators. "We have ten of these. The blast radius is five meters for each. We can toss these accurately and quickly and demolish this entire patrol in exactly five seconds."

"You'll blow yourself up," the Haariden captain sneered.

Obi-Wan smiled. "I don't think so."

The next thing the captain knew, Obi-Wan had somersaulted over his head and landed on his other side. "Maybe I need to remind you," Obi-Wan said. "We are Jedi."

The other Haariden soldiers looked nervous. They glared at one another, then at their captain.

"I'm not inclined to find out if they can do it," one soldier muttered.

"Why should we?" another said.

"This isn't even our fight," the first soldier added.

"Why can't we just return to our unit?" another asked.

The captain eyed the thermal detonator in Soara's hand, her thumb over the release.

"What happens to us?" he asked.

"We have no quarrel with you," Obi-Wan said. "As long as we have safe passage to our transport."

The captain paused. Then he slowly lowered his blaster.

Soara and Obi-Wan dropped the thermal detonators back into the pockets of their tunics.

"What do you mean, it's not your fight?" Soara asked.

"We were paid to split off from our unit and attack you," the captain said, wiping a weary hand across his forehead.

Soara and Obi-Wan exchanged a glance. "Who paid you?" Soara asked.

The captain looked evasive. "No one we knew. I mean, not a native Haariden. An outlander."

"His name?"

"He didn't say."

"What did he look like?"

The captain was about to answer, but a blank look came over his face. He shook his head several times. "Isn't that strange," he said. "I honestly don't remember."

A pulse began to beat inside Obi-Wan. He gripped the hilt of his lightsaber.

"What is he to you?" Soara asked. "I would think you would rather have the Jedi on your side."

The captain gave a sad smile. "The Jedi can't help us. We are perfectly capable of destroying ourselves. Yes, he gave me his name. It was Granta Omega."

The name only confirmed what Obi-Wan had already suspected. He had met Granta Omega before. Omega had hired a group of bounty hunters to hunt him down, as well as Anakin and another Jedi. Obi-Wan had still not found out why. He knew that Omega was not a Sith, but he collected Sith artifacts.

Omega was also a void, a person with enough power to appear so neutral as to fade from the memory of those who had met him. He did not have a Force-connection, but he had cunning. And for some reason, he despised the Jedi.

Obi-Wan was not surprised to run into Granta Omega again. But why here, and why now?

Suddenly the horizon lit up with a dull red glow.

"The battle has resumed," the captain said tiredly. "We should return to our unit." He hesitated. "Since you have spared our lives, I will also tell you this — all units have been called to the battle on the other edge of the forest. You will have no trouble reaching your transport safely. Our concerns now lie elsewhere." He bowed. "Captain Noq Welflet, at your service."

He looked at the soldiers, who had dropped back to

the ground. Some of them sat, their heads in their hands. Others looked numbly around.

"My soldiers are exhausted," he said. "I took the credits from Granta in order to feed and clothe them. I did not want to fight the Jedi. I do not want to fight at all, actually." He made an attempt at a laugh, but began to cough. "My lungs are full of smoke and ashes," he murmured.

"Why do you continue?" Obi-Wan asked.

Captain Welflet's eyes were red-rimmed above his straggly beard. "Because I must."

Soara raised a hand to take in the exhausted patrol, the ruined village, the blackened stumps. "And it's worth all this? Your land ruined, your people dead?"

The captain sighed. "I only know there is no alternative."

Obi-Wan and Soara headed back to the others. They were both saddened by their experience on Haariden. There seemed little chance for peace.

They hurried back to the group and told the scientists the good news. They should reach the transport without incident.

"And the Haariden patrol?" Anakin asked.

"They've gone back to join the war," Obi-Wan said. "They won't bother us." He would tell Anakin about

Granta Omega back at the Temple. Now they needed to focus on getting off-planet.

Soara and Obi-Wan fashioned a body sling and tied Darra gently against Obi-Wan's chest. They hiked to the transport, making good time now. The sky lightened and a pale sun rose as they reached the ship.

The scientists boarded with weary relief. Obi-Wan gently set Darra down on a sleep couch and covered her with a thermal blanket. Soara slid behind the controls. Obi-Wan contacted the Temple and said they were on their way.

They shot up into the upper atmosphere of Haariden. Obi-Wan looked down at the planet, glad to be leaving it. He wondered about the disturbance in the Force he had felt since he'd arrived. He had thought it was because of the dark side on this planet. There was so much death and bitterness. But what about his sense of foreboding? Could he have somehow picked up on the fact that Granta Omega was here as well?

The fact that Omega had failed in his attempt to kill the Jedi didn't matter. If Darra had not been ill, if he hadn't pledged to get the scientists to safety, he would have stayed with his Padawan and hunted down his attacker. Omega had tried to kill Jedi twice. He should be brought to justice.

But Obi-Wan had his duties, and he had to leave. He

had made the same decision on Ragoon-6. Justice would have to be sought another time. Could it be that Omega only attacked when he knew the Jedi could not retaliate or pursue him? Did he count on a Jedi's sense of priorities to protect himself from reprisals?

Obi-Wan turned away from the planet and looked ahead at the galaxy. The ship shot into hyperspace, and a rush of stars seemed to crowd the windscreen. This time, Obi-Wan vowed, he would get to the bottom of the mystery of Granta Omega.

CHAPTER SIX

Obi-Wan accessed the door to the Jedi Temple Archive Library and stopped in the doorway. Usually it was a pristine space with not a holofile out of place. Busts of great Jedi Masters lined one wall, and the soft glow of computer panels created a hushed atmosphere. Today it was in chaos.

Holofiles hung in the air while datasheets littered the usually empty counters. Jedi archivist Madame Jocasta Nu stood in the center of the room, two laser pointers stuck haphazardly in her gray wispy bun. Her small, nimble fingers flicked through one holofile after another.

She looked up at him, irritated. "In or out, young Jedi."

It never failed. Madame Jocasta Nu could make him

feel like a fifth-year student. She appeared frail but her authority was unquestionable.

She pulled out a laser pointer and frowned at it, then used it to make a correction in a file. "Well?"

Obi-Wan stepped inside. "Am I interrupting?"

"Of course you are. Cleaning day. I have to organize once a month. Retire old files, organize, send others to deep storage. Not a good day. It always puts me in a bad mood."

"Ah," Obi-Wan said, "well . . ."

"Which doesn't mean I'm not available," she said crisply. "Just that you won't get the benefit of my usual good humor."

"Ah," Obi-Wan said again. He had never enjoyed the benefit of Jocasta Nu's good humor. Perhaps he'd been at the other end of her private amusement at his failure to keep up with Senate subcommittee agendas. That was the only time he could remember her smiling at him. It hadn't been a very nice smile.

Jocasta Nu shook her head. "Oh, for star's sake, Master Kenobi, stop repeating yourself. What do you need?"

"Some time ago I asked you to research someone called Granta Omega. You assembled a file —"

"I remember."

"Which I need to review."

She sighed. "Today, I suppose?"

"I'm afraid so."

Jocasta Nu crossed the room and began to access a holofile directory. She hummed a tuneless melody while she tapped one finger on the counter. "Here we go. I can do a fresh search as well, if you like."

"That would be helpful."

She flipped through the file. "Though as I remember, this subject's problem was decentralization."

"What do you mean?" Obi-Wan asked.

"Scattered." Her slender fingers wiggled. "Spread out. Diluted."

"I understand what the word means, I just don't —"

"Sorry. One of my own classification terms. Some subjects are solid. You can look them up, research, find out what you need. Some are diffuse. They are spread out so far they almost disappear." She hummed under her breath. "This Omega was like that. Enormously wealthy, but no particular home. Many companies within companies within companies . . . many acquaintances, no friends. His business interests are galaxy-wide." She sent the holofile spinning through the air toward Obi-Wan. "You have a file full of information that tells you nothing."

Just like his physical appearance, Obi-Wan thought,

stopping the file with a raised hand. The man hid behind a blank wall he created himself.

He looked through the file again. Omega specialized in ferreting out rare minerals and buying the whole source, then raising the price. He was enormously wealthy yet kept his wealth diversified and hidden in any number of secret accounts. There was no information that either Obi-Wan or Jocasta Nu had been able to find on his beginnings. They did not know his home planet. He just suddenly appeared, a wealthy man.

Obi-Wan looked through the list of his known homes. There were fifteen of them spread over the galaxy. Tracking him down would be extremely difficult and time-consuming.

He closed the file and sent it back to Jocasta Nu. "I doubt you'll find anything, but if you could do a new search . . ."

She nodded. "I'll get back to you."

Just then Yoda appeared in the doorway. "Find you here, I am not surprised. It is still Omega you seek?"

Obi-Wan walked out to join him in the hallway. "It seems he is almost impossible to find."

"Impossible, nothing is. Difficult, many things are. To you the question must be, why search?"

"I have a feeling," Obi-Wan said. "Maybe it is up to

me to prevent something before it happens. I don't want to wait for disaster to overtake me."

Yoda nodded, his gray-blue eyes revealing nothing. "But an immediate threat Omega is not."

"The immediate threat is not always apparent."

"Argue with you I will not," Yoda said. "Your decision, this is. But think I do that you need a better reason to spend time on this. Heard I have that your Padawan needs you. Events on Haariden marked him, they have."

"Yes," Obi-Wan said. "He feels responsible for Darra's injury. She'll be fine, but she lost her lightsaber. He feels terrible about that. And I was not happy with his actions during the battle."

"Lightsaber skills, important they are," Yoda said. "How to use as well as how not to use. When to move as well as when not to move. Restraint, your young Padawan needs, as well as direction."

"I've spoken to him," Obi-Wan said. "He listens. Yet I've come to see that Anakin really learns by doing. With every mission, he grows."

"Yet sometimes one Knight is not enough to teach a Padawan," Yoda said. He paused. Obi-Wan knew he had more to say. They moved down the hall, Yoda's gimer stick tapping as he walked.

Yoda spoke as they reached the lift tube. "Hear I

have that Soara Antana will remain at the Temple until Darra is better."

"Yes, she will not leave her."

"Not much she has to do, I think," Yoda said. "Distraction, she needs." The lift tube opened and he stepped in. He nodded at Obi-Wan as the doors slid closed.

Obi-Wan smiled. He saw what Yoda was suggesting. "I think I know a way to keep her busy," he said to the closed doors.

CHAPTER SEVEN

Anakin sat in the map room. He had activated dozens of holographic worlds at once. They swirled around him in their varied systems while dozens of voices told him facts about their climate, geography, species, and culture. The voices blended into an indistinguishable babble.

It was an exercise he had invented to calm his mind. He drew the Force around him to help him concentrate. Then he tried to find the thread of one voice and follow it. As soon as he had, he would add another. He thought of the voices as layers in his mind, and he tried to keep track of what each voice was telling him, all at the same time. It was difficult and took tremendous concentration. But all the voices together filled up the space in his head and drowned out his own voice, his own feelings. So he would not have to think, only concentrate.

Concentration is different from thinking, his Master had told him. *When you are concentrating hard enough, you shouldn't be thinking at all.*

It was here in the map room that he had first understood what Obi-Wan had meant.

He was concentrating so intently on separating the voices that he didn't hear Obi-Wan come in. His Master could move without making the smallest sound, but Anakin wanted to reach the point where he always knew when Obi-Wan entered the room. He wasn't there yet.

Obi-Wan sat down beside him and waited for him to turn.

"A mission?" Anakin asked hopefully.

"No, we are at the Temple for a while," Obi-Wan said. "I haven't told you something I discovered on Haariden, something I told the Council about. That patrol was paid to attack us by Granta Omega."

Anakin felt the nerves inside his body tighten. He realized he had been waiting for this. He had wanted to pursue Omega after their experience on Ragoon-6.

"Why didn't you tell me before?"

"You had enough to think about."

Anakin knew that his Master meant his concern for Darra. He had haunted the med clinic until he knew she would fully recover.

"Are we going after him?" Anakin asked.

"Jocasta Nu is helping me do some research," Obi-Wan said. Anakin realized this wasn't quite an answer. "In the meantime," Obi-Wan continued, "I have something for you to do."

"I am ready, Master."

"I have arranged a private lightsaber tutorial for you with Soara Antana."

Anakin felt his heart fall. Shame filled him. "Because of what happened on Haariden."

"Yes," Obi-Wan said. "There is no blame, Padawan. Yet there are things you need to learn. Things that I have not been able to teach you."

"There is nothing you can't teach me, Master," Anakin argued. But the real reason for Anakin's disquiet was a secret fear that Obi-Wan planned to leave him behind while he went after Granta Omega. Obi-Wan would do the real work while he remained behind like a schoolboy, taking lessons.

"This is not your decision, Padawan." Obi-Wan's tone was sharp. "This is a great honor for you. Soara rarely takes individual students. She would not agree if she didn't think you had great potential."

Anakin fought with his feelings. He did not want to confess to his Master that he was afraid Obi-Wan would leave him. "Yes, Master."

The stern lines of Obi-Wan's face relaxed into a smile at Anakin's obedient tone. "You might have fun."

Anakin looked at him with such disbelief that Obi-Wan's smile turned into a laugh.

Later that afternoon, Anakin tucked the training lightsaber into his belt with distaste. He felt like a young student again. He found himself tugging at his tunic to straighten it before walking into the practice area to meet Soara. Quickly he rumpled it again. He wasn't a student any longer. He was a Padawan Learner.

Soara didn't notice his rumpled tunic or his lack of enthusiasm. She nodded shortly at him. "Let's go."

"Go?" Anakin was puzzled. Lightsaber training had always taken place in the practice room.

She lifted a corner of her mouth in a small smile. "Do you expect there to be a practice room to fight in on missions?"

Anakin grinned. "I guess not." Maybe he would enjoy this after all.

Soara took him to the landing platform, where he jumped into an airspeeder next to her. Her piloting was as aggressive and graceful as her battle form. She took him to a part of Coruscant he'd never visited, a hundred levels or so below the Temple. Here, an entire quarter of the city was being knocked down in order to build new construction. Half-demolished buildings were surrounded by blocks of duracrete, bundles of durasteel cables, and towers of polished stone blocks.

Soara parked the speeder and slid out. Anakin jumped out after her and looked around. The work had stopped for the day. The buildings threw deep jagged shadows over the walkways. There had once been an attempt to keep the walkways clean of debris, but the sweeping had been half completed and footing was treacherous. He waited to see what Soara would do.

Soara did nothing. She picked her way over to a building and looked up at the frame being erected. "Housing," she said. "Coruscant always needs more housing. Amazing that people keep immigrating here. Do you know that building is the biggest industry on Coruscant?"

Was he here for an economics lesson? "I didn't know."

He tilted his head back to follow her gaze, following the durasteel frame of the building. Suddenly a shadow off to his left moved, and a figure leaped through the air toward him. Anakin saw a blaze of orange. A lightsaber!

He just had time to jump back and fumble for his training lightsaber as he felt the sting of the blow against his forearm.

"Got ya," Tru Veld said, grinning. His friend had come at him from the high steel doorway behind him. He bounced back on his flexible legs and saluted Anakin with a lightsaber flourish. He, too, was using a training lightsaber — able to defend, but not to harm.

Confused, Anakin glanced at Soara, his lightsaber in his hand.

"Do you expect your attacker to announce himself?" she asked.

Tru came toward him again. Anakin somersaulted backward and then twisted to come at Tru from the left. He sliced the hem of Tru's tunic.

"Missed me," Tru said, dancing backward. His silver eyes gleamed. He was having fun.

Anakin reversed. His lightsaber hit Tru's. Smoke rose, and Anakin almost stumbled when Tru ducked and rushed at him, surprising him.

Tru might be having fun, but he was serious.

Anakin had barely missed being stung by Tru's blow. He emptied his mind of his surprise at Tru's appearance. He had to concentrate in order to gather in what he thought of as his battle mind. His attention expanded to include everything around him. And yet his focus was now entirely on Tru. Everything he knew about Tru clicked in and became information he could use.

Tru was a Teevan, and thus his limbs were more flexible than Anakin's.

Tru never played a game he wasn't certain he would win.

Tru's left hand was stronger than his right.

Tru liked to choose the rhythm of the battle.

Anakin moved to confuse and unsettle his friend. He fought aggressively, then stepped back to lure Tru forward. He landed a blow on Tru's arm.

Normally, a Jedi Master would announce points when blows were struck. The winning blow would be to the neck. Soara did not. He knew she was watching, but he tried not to think about it. Still, he felt her circling, watching them from every angle.

Anakin used the ground. While he moved, he noticed everything — the cables, the blocks of stone, the tiniest pebble on the ground, the hydrospanner abandoned on the top of a block of duracrete. Someone's lunch bucket left on a grassy area by the walkway. He drove Tru steadily backward. Tru suddenly leaped high above and grabbed a pole with only his legs. On his backward swing, he struck out at Anakin.

It was a surprising move, and Anakin hadn't expected it. His eyes gleamed as he leaped to avoid Tru. Tru swung around the pole twice while Anakin dodged, wedged between a half-built wall and a deep pit. He slashed at Tru, who suddenly leaped off the pole and landed behind Anakin.

Perfect. Anakin whirled and drove Tru back onto the grass. Tru's foot hit the lunch bucket and he stumbled. His lightsaber was in his left hand from his twirl around the pole, and Anakin saw it wobble.

It was time for Anakin to move in with the killing blow, the sting of the training lightsaber. All he had to do was step forward and lightly touch Tru's neck.

But he hated to win the battle based on a moment of awkwardness on Tru's part, even if he himself had engineered it. He would embarrass his friend in front of Soara Antana. Instead, he hesitated a fraction of a second, long enough for Tru to regain some sense of balance. Then they fought on.

The moon was rising and they were both drenched in sweat when Soara called a halt. "Let's call it a draw."

Anakin slipped the lightsaber into his belt, satisfied. He knew he had fought well. Tru brought out the best in him.

"You can go, Tru," Soara said. "Thank you."

Tru grinned at Anakin. "Good fight. See you back at the Temple."

Soara did not move. Anakin stood, breathing heavily, waiting for her critique. He knew a few places where he could have fought better. She would not say anything that would surprise him.

"I called it a draw, but you lost," Soara said. "And you lost in the worst sort of way."

Anakin looked at her with new attention, surprised. "What?"

"If you want to become great, you must fight without emotion," Soara said. "You obviously have not learned this. You must fight without anger, without fear, without rage. Without ego."

"Without ego? But —"

"No buts. Listen. On Haariden, you made the same mistake. Because you know Darra, you rushed in to protect her. Today you protected Tru. You think you are doing this as a mark of friendship. But you're really doing it to boost your own ego."

"My own ego?" Anakin was astonished.

Soara crossed her arms. "You know, Anakin, things will go a lot faster if you don't repeat everything I say. Yes, your own ego. You think you're a better fighter than your friends. You think you're faster. You think you need to go easy on them. Let me tell you something. You're not better. As a matter of fact, you're a good deal worse."

The words stung. Anakin felt his face grow hot. The evening wind was cool and drying his sweat.

Soara whirled and kicked backward at his hand. He did not even feel the blow, but his lightsaber was suddenly shooting out of his hand and clattering to the stone pavement.

"And another thing," she said. "Never let down your guard."

Anakin picked up the hilt of the lightsaber and stuck it in his belt. He vowed to himself that Soara Antana would not take him by surprise again. He would use what she gave him. He would absorb her hard words and her lessons. By the end of this tutorial, he would change her opinion about him. He would be the best Padawan she'd ever taught.

He slipped into the med clinic. The light tubes were powered down to a soft glow. He walked as quietly as he could to the side of Darra's med couch. She looked small and helpless, still hooked up to monitoring machines. Her eyes were closed.

Her mouth curved into a smile. "Hello, Anakin," she said without opening her eyes.

"I came to say good night. Are you feeling better?"

"Yes. Much." She opened her eyes and glanced at

him. "Better than you look, anyway. What have you been doing?"

"A private tutorial with your Master."

She gave a sympathetic groan. "Ooh. Sorry."

He crouched down so that they were at eye level. "She's very tough."

"The toughest."

"But I can learn."

"If you listen. She'll push you hard, and then she'll tell you something strange, something you don't want to understand. That's what she wants. The more tired you are, the emptier you are. That's when she really starts to work."

"Lucky me," Anakin said with a grimace. "Look, I'm sorry about what happened on Haariden. She told me it was my ego. She was right."

"It's okay," Darra said. "Now I have something to impress the younger kids with. I was wounded in battle."

"I'm here to make you a promise," Anakin said.

"Don't," Darra said, rising on her elbows. "I know what you're going to say, and you can't promise such a thing. Besides, I can get my lightsaber back myself."

"But I'm the reason you lost it."

"*I'm* the reason I lost it," Darra said firmly. "I'm the one who dropped it. Did you ever think it was your ego that wants to get it back?" Suddenly she slumped against the pillow. "Do me a favor. Don't argue with me. I'm too tired."

Anakin saw the exhaustion in her face she had tried to hide. "Is there anything I can do for you? Would you like some juice, or some food, or some music?"

Darra's eyelids fluttered closed. "Just one thing," she said. "Stay with me until I fall asleep. It's lonely here."

"I will." Anakin shifted his weight so that he was sitting on the floor. He leaned against the sleep couch next to her head. He knew she could feel the pressure of his body, and that would make her feel safe. He sat there until her breathing slowed and he knew she was asleep.

"I promise you, Darra," he whispered. "I will return your lightsaber to you. It is not my ego. It is my promise."

CHAPTER EIGHT

Obi-Wan hurried into the library. It had been restored to its usual pristine state. Jocasta Nu was at a datascreen, working.

"What is it?" she asked, looking up for a moment and then back down at her screen.

"You sent for *me*," Obi-Wan said.

"Right." Jocasta clicked off the screen. "I have good news and bad news. Good news — I found out Granta Omega's listed birthplace. It's Coruscant."

"Coruscant?" Obi-Wan grew excited. That meant he could investigate a good deal of Omega's background without leaving the planet. A being's records were always stored on his or her home planet, and Coruscant was especially careful about storing every scrap of information. Thousands were employed in record-keeping.

Then he rem[...] Jocasta had said there was bad news as we[...]

"I can find n[...] of his birth. Nothing. And you know Coruscant [...] organized about these things. So either he lied [...] as born somewhere else, or he lives under an as[...] name."

"In other word[...] know nothing more," Obi-Wan said, sinking down [...] hair. "Every time I think I have a lead, it disappea[...] left with nothing."

Suddenly holof[...] egan to zoom from Jocasta's fingers toward him.

"What is this?" [...] an said.

"You say you ha[...] othing on Omega," she said. "I'm showing you dif[...] ntly."

"But I've already s[...] these. They don't say anything!"

"They say many t[...] s," Jocasta said, exasperated. "You just can't put th[...] ces together."

Obi-Wan almost s[...] d. Jocasta reminded him of Qui-Gon. What would [...] aster say if he were here?

Qui-Gon had always [...] n better at research, at putting pieces together. H[...] always able to connect the dry facts with the living [...] on. That would lead him to motives and reasons, [...] oon he would have a picture of what he was loo[...] or.

What is the emotion [...]? he would say. What does this being want more tha[...] ything? What does he need?

How am I supposed to know that, Qui-Gon?

"Start with what you know for sure," Obi-Wan suddenly blurted. "That's what Qui-Gon always said."

Jocasta sniffed. "Exactly."

"I know he has a vendetta against the Jedi," Obi-Wan said. "He hates us. I know he was on Haariden." Obi-Wan straightened. "I know he was on Haariden!" he repeated. "And it couldn't have been because the Jedi were there. It would have been impossible for him to plan the attack beforehand."

"Not impossible," Jocasta corrected. "There is little that is impossible."

Now she sounded like Yoda. "But we received the summons and left within one hour," Obi-Wan said. "Improbable, then. No, I think he was on Haariden for another reason. When he discovered the Jedi were there, he saw a way to make trouble for us." He began to search randomly through the holofiles. "He made his fortune by buying up minerals on different worlds and creating shortages," he said. "We know that, too."

"Let me get the file on Haariden," Jocasta said. Her eyes were alight with interest now. She quickly accessed a file and began to flip through it. "Interesting. Do you know why the two factions on Haariden have been fighting this time?"

"Land disputes," Obi-Wan said.

"Yes, but this isn't about territory. It's about what is *underneath* the land. Traces of titanite have been found."

"Titanite? I don't think I know it."

"That's because it's extremely rare," Jocasta said. "Not only that, it's very hard to mine. It's usually buried so deep near the core that it costs more to extract it than it is worth."

"What is it used for?" Obi-Wan asked.

"Until recently, not much," Jocasta said. "But in the last couple of years, it's been discovered that when titanite is synthesized, a substance is extracted that is one of the essential ingredients of bacta."

Obi-Wan shook his head. "Bacta . . ." He began to flip through the files in front of him. "Here it is. One of Omega's vast land holdings is on the planet Thyferra. That's the only place where the alazhi plant grows. Alazhi lotion is the main ingredient in bacta."

"So if he had alazhi lotion and the titanite substance . . ." Jocasta said, her voice trailing off.

Obi-Wan and Jocasta stared at each other as the conclusion struck them.

"He could corner the galactic market on bacta," Obi-Wan said.

"This is getting very interesting," Jocasta murmured.

"When was the titanite found on Haariden?" Obi-Wan asked.

"Only a few months ago," Jocasta said. "That's why the fighting began again. It's also one of the reasons the scientists were sent there. Haariden was included on the mapping expedition for precisely that reason. The Senate felt that if it had a complete picture of where the titanite deposits were, it could persuade the two sides to come to an agreement."

"Did the scientists make a final report?"

"Yes, but it was inconclusive. They couldn't conduct the tests they needed to because the fighting moved too close."

"Maybe Omega wanted that to happen," Obi-Wan said. "Maybe he didn't want the report to get back to the Senate."

"He would need to make his own tests, then," Jocasta said. "He'd need to have his own scientific team. That would be a hard thing to keep secret on Haariden."

"Maybe he didn't need a team," Obi-Wan said. "Maybe he could do it himself." He waved at the holofiles surrounding them. "Think about it. Look at what he's done over the years. Look at the fact that he doesn't employ many people at all. It would have been impossible for Omega to have done what he did in his career without some serious scientific knowledge. Which means," he said, turning to Jocasta excitedly, "he would have to have had some serious study. Can you search the records of the finest scientific institutes in the galaxy?"

Jocasta raised an eyebrow. "All of them?"

Obi-Wan nodded.

"I'll start with the Core Worlds," she said with a sigh. "Maybe we'll get lucky."

Obi-Wan was sipping a cup of tea in the Room of a Thousand Fountains and trying to calm his mind when his comlink signaled. It was Jocasta.

"He attended the All Science Research Academy on Yerphonia," she said.

"Can we contact them?" Obi-Wan asked eagerly.

"I already have. He was granted his degree only seven years ago. He was a star student. His home world is a small moon called Nierport Seven."

Obi-Wan knew the place. It was less than a day's travel from Coruscant.

Within an hour, he was on his way.

CHAPTER NINE

"Again," Soara said.

Anakin ran at the wall again. He no longer knew how many times he had done so. Fifty? Seventy? Two hundred, five hundred? His brain didn't register numbers. There was just him and the wall.

He ran up the wall, flipped over into a backward somersault, and landed on his feet again. It was a basic Temple exercise. He'd learned it when he was nine. But with Soara he was discovering that it was a much more complex maneuver than he'd imagined. Apparently his shoulders were wrong. His landing was too hard. And the whole thing took too long for him to accomplish.

"Stop." Soara's voice cut through him like the cold wind that howled down the deserted alley straight to the secluded lot where they were training. The building in front of him was sheer durasteel, slippery now with morning dew. The sun was just rising.

"Close your eyes," Soara said.

Anakin closed his eyes.

"Get rid of that impatience," Soara said. "Now."

Anakin tried to obey.

"Nothing is solid," Soara said. "The hardest wall is just a connection of particles. Find the spaces between the particles, and the wall will yield. It will push you off. Listen to the wall and hear the wind through the gaps."

Listen to the wall? Anakin felt his impatience rise again.

He remembered Darra's words. *She'll push you hard, and then she'll tell you something strange, something you don't want to understand. That's what she wants. The more tired you are, the emptier you are. That's when she really starts to work.*

He listened to the wall. And then the sound of the wind changed. He heard the howl of it, but he also heard the whisper. He heard it stir a piece of trash on the street, disturb a pebble. And then he heard it whistle softly through the gaps. Nothing felt solid. Not the ground under his feet, not the buildings around him.

He felt the Force move, even though he hadn't summoned it. He saw the wall in his mind, and this time, it shimmered. It wasn't a solid thing. It would yield to him.

He ran at the wall. He ran easily, as if it were the first time. He felt the wall give against his boots. He pushed off and the wall sprang against him, helping him propel. He somersaulted and flew backward, landing lightly, gracefully, his lightsaber held at the ready.

He blinked. He had fought with the help of the Force before. But never like that.

He looked at Soara, amazed.

She didn't smile or nod or show by even a flicker of an eyelash that she was pleased. But she didn't correct him, and that meant something. Anakin made sure his own pleasure didn't show on his face.

"That's enough for today," she said crisply.

Anakin deactivated his lightsaber. For the first time, he felt that he had glimpsed a future in which his connection to the Force and his lightsaber skills would be so meshed that he would truly be the best he could be. He could also see how far he was from that goal, but it didn't bother him as it would have the day before. He would get there.

They had walked to the training site, and Soara had already left for the Temple. She rarely said good-bye. Anakin looked down at his tunic and made a face. There was a ragged tear down the side, and it was stained with sweat and filth. He had already gone through five tunics since he'd begun training with Soara.

He started to trudge toward the lift tube that would bring him to the Senatorial level. From there he could take a series of connecting walkways to the Temple. It would be good to walk and see the morning bustle begin. He felt as though he had been facing nothing but a blank wall for hours.

Anakin grinned. He had.

Soara seemed to know every hidden corner of the seamier side of Coruscant. Over the past few days he'd climbed over junk heaps and through half-demolished buildings, crawled through tunnels, and even fought a battle with training droids in an airspeeder garage. He'd fallen into a vat of oil. That was a lesson he wouldn't forget.

Anakin zoomed up on the turbolift with a crowd of workers. At least he was too tired to dwell on his disappointment that Obi-Wan had left for Nierport Seven without him. His Master had assured him that he was going only for research purposes. When and if Obi-Wan decided to pursue Granta Omega, he would bring his Padawan with him. Obi-Wan had promised that.

Yet Anakin knew that Obi-Wan might run into surprises on Nierport Seven. He might find a clue he had to pursue immediately. He might not have time to send for Anakin. He could be left behind after all.

There was nothing he could do about it, however. The turbolift doors opened and Anakin stepped out, carried along with the crowd for a few steps until he broke away. The sun was rising now, the pink rays flashing on the cruisers in the space lanes and the buildings surrounding him.

He chose the least crowded walkway, the one that would bring him down the center of the fountains that lined one quadrant of the Senate complex. The coolness of the water freshened the air. He felt the droplets hit his skin. His weariness lifted, and he began to think about the morning meal ahead of him at the Temple.

A man sat on the edge of the fountain, his face lifted toward the spray. Then he turned and saw Anakin and waved.

For a moment, Anakin couldn't place him. Then he realized it was Tic Verdun, one of the scientists from Haariden. Verdun was now dressed in a cloak made of deep blue veda cloth. He looked completely different from the weary scientist he had met on Haariden.

"I'm so glad to see you!" Tic said, hurrying toward Anakin. "At this exact moment I was thinking of you. I didn't want to be forward, but I was wishing I could go to the Temple and inquire about the young girl."

"Darra will be fine," Anakin said. "The blaster bolts carried a chemical compound, but the medics were able to find the antidote."

"That's good news," Tic said warmly. "I will see the others at the hearing, and they'll be happy to hear it, too. We've submitted our final report and now we have to answer questions from the committee." He sighed. "Too bad the expedition ended badly. We didn't get to do the experiments on Haariden that we hoped. We could have put a stop to that bloody civil war if we had."

"How?" Anakin asked.

"The two tribes are fighting over possible titanite deposits," Tic explained. "If we had found exactly where the titanite was and how much there was, the Senate might have been able to come up with a plan to divide it equally. Instead, the two tribes are fighting over something that might not even exist."

"That's too bad," Anakin said.

Tic nodded, discouraged. "The worst part of it is, there was another scientist on Haariden who was also conducting experiments. If we could talk to him, maybe he had found out more. But nobody can seem to locate him."

"Another scientist? Who?" Anakin asked.

"Granta Omega," Tic Verdun said. "We ran into him on Haariden."

"You mean you know him?" Anakin asked, amazed.

Tic nodded. "Not well. But I've met him several times." He noted the interest on Anakin's face. "Why do you ask?"

"Because we're looking for him," Anakin said. "The Jedi would like to talk to him, too."

"Popular fellow." Tic frowned. "You know, I'm here on Coruscant with a group of friends. Some of them are scientists, some involved in business. We're having a kind of reunion. Most of them know Omega, too. Or they've met him, at least. Maybe if we put our heads together, we could come up with a lead for you. There's a chance we could know things you don't know."

"That wouldn't be hard," Anakin said ruefully. "We don't know much."

"I'll talk to them and see if I can come up with anything," Tic said. "They would be happy to help the Jedi, I am sure."

Anakin agreed enthusiastically. He said good-bye to Tic and hurried toward the Temple. He wouldn't contact Obi-Wan about this, he decided. Not yet. First he would compile information.

Wouldn't it be amazing if he were to be the one to find Granta Omega?

CHAPTER TEN

Nierport Seven was within the Core, but its desolation reminded Obi-Wan of an Outer Rim planet. It was a cold, barren moon with only one small settlement. Nierport's meager vegetation appeared to be a wild bush with red thorns well over a meter long. It was said the bushes bloomed with beautiful violet flowers in the summer, but the summer only lasted a month. The rest of the year was numbingly cold and bleak. The buildings were built with thick blocks of stone designed to keep out the cold wind.

Nierport Seven was one of seven moons in a small system that was notable only because it was a convenient refueling stop on the way to Coruscant. Most of the intragalactic travelers chose to refuel on the planet

Eeropha, which at least had several small cities. But Nierport Seven was able to support a refueling stop of its own and a few small guesthouses, all serving the kind of pilots who could not afford to scrounge up even the low prices Eeropha charged.

At least the moon was small, Obi-Wan told himself. The population was clustered around the refueling station. It did not take him long to locate several people who had known Granta Omega.

That was the good news. The bad news was that no one knew very much about him.

There was only one café on Nierport Seven, and it was next to the refueling station. The café was called Food and Drink, and the owner turned out to be as cut and dry as the title of his establishment.

"Never knew him personally. Heard of him. He left." That was all the owner had to say.

"Is there anyone else who would know him?" Obi-Wan asked. "Anybody who still lives here? He left seven years ago."

"Most folks leave in three years," the owner said. "Can't take any more."

Obi-Wan waited. He had learned this from Qui-Gon. Most beings would come up with additional information if you just stayed quiet.

"Might try that trio in the corner," the owner said

gruffly. "They've stuck around. They were born here and they'll die here."

The three natives of Nierport sat around the table. They were wearing grease-stained clothes that told Obi-Wan they had just finished a shift at the refueling station.

Obi-Wan nodded a hello. They looked at him warily.

"Jedi?" one of them said. "Never seen your kind here."

Obi-Wan eyed their empty glasses. "Anyone for a re-fill?"

Their empty glasses were pushed away and they looked at him hopefully. Obi-Wan signaled for another round. "And I'll have the same," he told the bartender.

The drinks arrived. They clinked the smeared glasses.

Obi-Wan peered at the red liquid. "What is this?"

"Claing juice," one of the men said. "It's native to the system. We extract the juice from the thorns of the native bush."

Obi-Wan took a small sip. The juice seared his lips and tongue and then burned like blazing fire going down. He managed not to cough, but his eyes streamed tears.

The three men laughed uproariously.

"Claing can even bring a Jedi to his knees," one of them chortled.

"I'll say," Obi-Wan choked out.

His streaming eyes and burning throat were worth it. He had passed a test. The trio decided to befriend him. He asked about Granta Omega, and they nodded.

"He was a boy when he left," one said. "Went to study somewhere, I think. His mother Tura died two years later. He never came back to see her."

"Not even for the funeral," someone else said.

"What about his father?" Obi-Wan asked.

"Never knew him," the first man said. "Tura Omega showed up one day, got a job at the refueling station, had this three-year-old boy. Nobody asks questions on Nierport Seven."

"Except for Jedi," another one said, and this caused them great amusement.

"I could show you his house," the first man offered. He licked his lips. "I could use another claing, though."

"I'll buy you one afterward," Obi-Wan said.

They walked out into the numbing cold. The ground was brittle with frost. They walked through the main street and then turned down a smaller road. It wasn't far to the outskirts of the settlement. The man pointed to a small house. It looked no different from the others. It was built with rounded walls and seemed to hunch against the wind.

"That there is his house. A space pilot owns it now.

Uses it on stopovers. Lots of pilots do that here. It's cheap and convenient."

Obi-Wan peered into the window. The house was empty except for a stove and a bedroll. The room was small and low-ceilinged. Even with furniture it would look bleak. There was nothing to see here. There was nothing to learn. It was typical of his search for Granta Omega.

"You said his mother worked at the refueling station?" Obi-Wan asked. "Did she have a good job?"

The man laughed. "If you call hauling lubricant hoses around all day for no money a good job."

"So how did she manage to send her son to study off-planet?" Obi-Wan wondered.

"She had nothing to do with it," the man said. "The boy had brilliance. Everybody knew that. She found him a sponsor on Eeropha. He sent him to a scientific institute."

"Do you know who the sponsor was?" Obi-Wan asked. "Does he still live on Eeropha?"

"He lives on Coruscant now. Big fancy person now. He's the Senator from Eeropha. Name is Sano Sauro," the man said.

Obi-Wan felt a chill. He knew Sano Sauro. He was once a prosecutor. Ten years before, Obi-Wan had to undergo an investigation into a fellow Padawan's death.

Sauro had grilled him mercilessly about Bruck Chun's fall.

Obi-Wan had since found peace about Bruck's death, but he wasn't looking forward to meeting up with Sauro again.

He pressed some credits in the man's hand. "Thank you. Buy your friends another claing."

The man grinned. "Sure you don't want to join us?"

Obi-Wan winced. "I don't think I'd survive."

The man took off. Obi-Wan looked down the street, then across the frozen wasteland. He could understand a boy wanting to leave this place. He could understand how poverty might mark him. But why Granta Omega wished harm on the Jedi, he still didn't know. He had a feeling that if he solved that mystery, he would find the man.

CHAPTER ELEVEN

Anakin had expected that after his breakthrough his next practice session with Soara would bring him to the next level. Instead, she had him do more simple drills. At least this time he did not have to leave the Temple.

He had to activate his lightsaber from different positions, again and again. He had to practice a midair thrust. He had to practice a double reversal. He had to practice moves he had done a thousand times before.

Not once did Soara mention the spaces between particles, or concentration, or the Force. She just repeated, "Again," over and over until he thought he would break his lightsaber hilt in two.

And then the session was finished. Anakin leaned over, trying to catch his breath. Disappointment swelled in him and he felt as though he were choking on it.

After getting a glimpse of the fighter he could be, he was reduced to being a student again.

He slammed his training lightsaber back in his belt. What he needed was something to eat and a fresh tunic. He took the long way back to his quarters in order to compose himself.

The illumination banks were mimicking dusk as he passed by the lake. The green water looked inviting. The splash of the waterfall in the deep pool was tinted pink. He thought about taking a quick swim, but he was too hungry. Soara had kept him a long time, and he had missed the midday meal. He had a feeling she had kept him deliberately. She wanted him to feel hungry and empty. She wanted to see how far he could push himself. He hoped he had passed the test.

Then he realized that his test was yet to come.

He was tired. So tired that he almost missed the blur at the corner of his vision. A lightsaber had been activated and someone hurled at him from a tree branch above. It was another one of Soara's sudden attacks. She had enlisted another Padawan to surprise him.

Anakin forgot his fatigue and jumped back just in time. To his dismay, he saw that his attacker was Ferus Olin.

If only it had been anyone else! Anakin didn't like to

see Ferus under the best of circumstances. He certainly didn't want to fight him when he was tired and hungry.

Soara appeared on top of the waterfall where she could watch. He knew he had no choice. As Ferus came at him with a somersaulting reversal, Anakin kicked into fight mode. She had sent the best Padawan fighter in the Temple against him. She wanted to see what he would do.

He would win.

What Soara could not know was that this time, friendship would not gentle him. Not with Ferus.

Ferus was starting out slowly. He would fight smart. He would save his energy and pace himself. Anakin decided to surprise him.

He launched an assault so fierce that he saw Ferus's eyes flare with astonishment. Ferus retreated fast, needing to collect himself. Anakin came after him, swinging his training lightsaber without pause. He almost touched him, but Ferus twisted away just in time, turning the movement into a twisting leap. He surprised Anakin by immediately swinging back a backward blow. Anakin ducked, feeling the whistle of air created by the power of Ferus's swipe.

Ferus was tall and solid, but he was also agile.

He was expert at using the ground.

Unlike Tru, he used both hands equally well.

The rocky terrain was perfect for his style.

He jumped, spun, and leaped, keeping Anakin off guard. Now he was driving the battle. Anakin did not know how Ferus had regained the upper hand, but he wasn't happy about it. He was reacting to Ferus's moves instead of the other way around. What was Soara thinking?

Anakin feinted to his left and then leaped straight ahead. To his dismay, Ferus dropped to the floor and rolled underneath Anakin, then sprang up in one smooth movement. He was behind him now. Anakin had only a split second before he felt the touch of the lightsaber on his shoulder. It only just missed his neck. When he twisted away, he saw the gleam of triumph in Ferus's eyes.

Fury roared through him. Ferus wanted to humiliate him in front of Soara!

He did something Ferus would never expect him to do. He copied Ferus's move, dropping to his knees and rolling underneath him as he made his next leap. He flipped up onto his feet and then charged at the rock wall.

The Force entered him. He felt it. He saw the rock wall as a shifting shape, ready to receive him. He sprang off the wall and straight over Ferus's head. It seemed the easiest thing in the galaxy to simply lean down and touch the side of Ferus's neck with his lightsaber.

He landed and looked up. Soara had seen everything. He had never fought so well.

She called down from the cliff, "Thank you, Ferus. Stay there, Anakin."

"Good fight," Ferus said, sticking the training lightsaber in his belt. "Except for one thing."

"What one thing?" Anakin asked, irritated. He wiped the sweat off his forehead with his sleeve.

Ferus only smiled. Then he walked off.

Anakin jammed the lightsaber hilt into his belt. No one could get to him like Ferus could.

Soara walked toward him. "That was your last lesson," she said.

Anakin was surprised and pleased. She must have seen how seamlessly he had connected with the Force.

"Before this, I had been impressed with your gifts," Soara said. "I had thought you had the potential to be one of the great Jedi fighters of all time. I thought I could teach you. Now I have grave doubts about you, Anakin."

Anakin couldn't believe what he was hearing. "What did I do wrong?"

"That question is the problem," Soara said, shaking

her head. "That is what is wrong. You don't know what you did. Didn't you feel your anger, Anakin? Didn't you realize it was fueling the battle?"

"Obi-Wan told you that Ferus and I do not get along," Anakin said sullenly.

"Obi-Wan didn't need to tell me," Soara snapped. "I saw it. Not from Ferus. From you."

"He wanted to win," Anakin said. "I saw triumph in his eyes when he surprised me."

"And it made you angry." Soara sighed. "Ferus did not fight from his emotion, Anakin. If you saw triumph in his eyes, he absorbed it and went on. That is the lesson you must learn. You will feel the emotion. You must let it go."

To his surprise, she suddenly strode forward and grabbed him by the shoulders. "You must do this, Anakin. You must learn this lesson. It is the most important one of all."

He didn't know what to say. He could promise her that he would learn it, but his promise would mean nothing. He knew that as a Jedi only his actions would convince her.

"Thank you for the time you devoted to teaching me," he said.

She dropped her hands. Now sadness was in her

eyes. That was the worst thing of all. "Go get something to eat."

Soara left, heading for the turbolift. Anakin walked over to the lake. He knelt by the deep pool created by the waterfall. He ducked his head into the cold water and came up spraying droplets that shined like bright gems in the light created by the illumination banks overhead.

He would not let this bother him, he told himself fiercely. He had made a mistake. Soara should have understood that. He was a Padawan, not a Jedi. Of course he would make mistakes. It wasn't fair.

She said she had her doubts that he would make a great Jedi. Yet she had seen the potential for it. He would surprise her. He would surprise them all.

He rose and headed away from the lake. He would start by surprising Obi-Wan. Thanks to Tic Verdun, he would locate Granta Omega.

CHAPTER TWELVE

Upon his return to Coruscant, Obi-Wan didn't stop at the Temple, but went right to the Senate. He paused inside the massive grand hall and accessed the directional system. He entered Sano Sauro's name and a map instantly appeared, highlighting the quickest route to his office. He would have to snake through several wings of the Senate complex. The system would print out a map on a durasheet, but Obi-Wan didn't need it. He memorized the route and took off.

Ever since he'd come here as a Jedi student, he had seen a Senate bustling with beings from all over the galaxy, but lately the halls had seemed even more crowded. The Senators' staffs were bloated with consorts, advisors, clerks, secretaries, assistants, and droids. Committees and subcommittees were tied up in hearings that stretched on for months, and sometimes years. Obi-Wan had always found Senators to admire for their dedication, but it was getting harder. The Senate continued to legislate, but it took more and more effort and time to get the smallest things done. Coalitions were formed, favors traded, credits amassed. Betrayals caused grudges that resulted in deep rifts that lasted for years. It was a different place than he had known.

Yet he continued to serve it. He did not think it was possible to have peace in the galaxy without it.

What kind of Senator was Sano Sauro? He did not want to make judgments before meeting him again. He had not seen him in ten years. Beings changed with time. He had known an ambitious lawyer who had attacked the Jedi and mocked the Force. Perhaps Sauro had found peace in a life of service. Obi-Wan would not expect trouble. He would hope for the best.

Still, he was uncomfortably aware of how deeply Sano Sauro had unnerved him as a young Padawan. The man's reserve had been icy. He did not seem to be able to speak without a sneer. Obi-Wan had felt that whatever he said to the prosecutor was wrong or foolish. He was a Jedi Knight now, and not easily intimidated. It would be interesting to see what the encounter would be like if Sano Sauro had not changed.

Obi-Wan reached the offices of Sano Sauro and

strode inside. A team of assistants worked busily at their desks. An ornate carved door led to an inner office. Obi-Wan told the receptionist his name and requested a few minutes of the Senator's time. He wondered if Sano Sauro would remember him.

He did not have to wonder long. The door hissed open and Sauro stood in the doorway. He looked oddly the same. He still had the same unlined face, the skin smooth and stretched tightly over the bones. His hair was still jet black. He could even have been dressed in the same clothes, a long black tunic and trousers. Obi-Wan could see small evidence of vanity in his brightly shined expensive boots.

"Obi-Wan Kenobi," he said through tight lips. "Don't tell me you've killed another Padawan."

He had not changed at all.

Obi-Wan was glad to note that Sano Sauro's words had not made even the slightest impression on him. He did not feel stung. He did not care what such a man thought of him. The opinion of a cruel man was worth less than nothing.

"I come on another matter and would welcome your help," Obi-Wan said.

Sano Sauro stepped aside. Obi-Wan took this as an invitation to enter the office. The door hissed shut behind him.

Sano Sauro sat behind a long, low desk built of stone. Two massive red thorns marked the corners. Obi-Wan recognized them from the claing bush.

Sauro said nothing but waited for him to begin. Obi-Wan remembered that, too. The prosecutor had never wasted time on pleasantries.

"I am trying to locate a protégé of yours called Granta Omega," Obi-Wan said. He waited to see if Sano Sauro would react to the name, but he did not. "Do you still know him?"

"He is a personal friend," Sano Sauro said.

"Can you tell me how I could contact him?"

"Why?"

"In connection with a Jedi matter," Obi-Wan said.

"Why would I give you any information?" Sano Sauro asked.

Now it was Obi-Wan's turn to say nothing. The rudeness was not unexpected.

"Because you ask?" Sauro said, folding his hands in front of him. "Because you are a Jedi?"

"Because there is no reason not to," Obi-Wan said. "And if there is, I would be interested in uncovering it. I would expect that an investigation into the reason would not please you."

"How interesting it must be to be a Jedi," Sano Sauro said. "You can bully and threaten and yet hide behind your robes and your talk of justice and the Force. Very convenient."

"I am not threatening you," Obi-Wan said evenly. "I asked you a legitimate question, which you refused to answer. I am interested in why."

"In that case, let me save you time. I am refusing to answer because I do not help the Jedi. It is as simple as that. The Senate in its collective delusion thinks we need you. I do not."

The door hissed open behind Obi-Wan. Sauro rose.

"I think I have come to the end of my patience," he said. "Good-bye."

The hatred in his gaze was no longer surprising to Obi-Wan. Sano Sauro had hated the Jedi ten years before and still hated them.

He could go over Sano Sauro's head. He could get the Jedi Council involved. They could go to Supreme Chancellor Palpatine. It was something to consider. If Granta Omega was planning to corner the market on bacta, the Chancellor would want to know.

Obi-Wan walked out of the inner office. The door hissed shut behind him. The assistants did not even glance at him. They sat hunched over their datascreens or talking on comlinks.

The assistant closest to Sauro's inner office was distractedly speaking on a comlink while entering data into a datapad. "No, we're not releasing copies," he said. "The expedition was cut short and the report was inconclusive. Senator Sauro has been thoroughly briefed. No, I won't put you through. Check with the Senate archivist, the Senator doesn't have time." The assistant cut the connection. "Journalists," he muttered.

"Was Senator Sauro on the committee that oversaw the mapping expedition that ended on Haariden?" Obi-Wan asked.

"Senator Sauro *headed* the committee," the assistant said haughtily.

Obi-Wan hurried from the room. He headed straight to the Senate archives, where committee records were kept. He filled out a request and waited impatiently until the information flashed onto his screen.

Obi-Wan's least favorite thing to do was wade through the minutes of Senatorial committee meetings. But he leaned forward, quickly scanning the report with interest. The decision to fund the mapping expedition took endless debate. Then names of scientists were submitted and debated. At last the team was decided on. Obi-Wan read the names and qualifications. Dr. Fort Turan. Joveh D'a Alin. Reug Yucon. Talie Heathe. And finally, Tic Verdun. He had been added at the last minute on the suggestion of the committee head, Senator Sauro . . .

Obi-Wan remembered something Talie Heathe had said on Haariden. Tic had been the scout. That meant he had been able to get away from the group for hours at a time.

Obi-Wan scanned Verdun's qualifications. He had graduated from the same scientific institute in the same year as Granta Omega.

He activated his comlink and contacted Jocasta Nu at the Temple.

"Please run a text doc identification search on Tic Verdun," he said.

He switched off the screen and hurried out of the archive room. He knew Jocasta Nu would not take long to answer him. He started back toward the Temple. By the time he reached the front doors, Jocasta Nu had signaled him.

"Interesting," Jocasta Nu said. "I just did a preliminary search, you understand. But the only information I can find is that he recently served on a Senatorial expedition to Haariden —"

"I know that. I met him there, remember?"

"And his credentials don't check out at all. If I had to guess, I'd say this was an alias. Strange that the Senate committee didn't pick it up."

"Not if the head of the Senate committee was his sponsor."

"Ah. Yes. There's a strange coincidence, though. He is listed as having a degree from the same school that —"

"— Granta Omega attended," Obi-Wan interrupted. Jocasta had told him everything he needed to know, which was nothing.

And now he knew that Tic Verdun was Granta Omega. He had met Omega on Ragoon-6. He had met a man whose face was disfigured with synth-flesh. His eyes had been gray. Obi-Wan could not connect that memory with Tic Verdun, with his shock of dark hair and his youthful face. Yet he was positive the two men were the same.

He stepped onto the lift tube and went straight to Anakin's quarters, but Anakin wasn't there. Obi-Wan tracked down Soara Antana, who was visiting Darra in the med center.

"Do you know where Anakin is?" he asked her.

"We had our practice session this morning," she said. "Then he headed off for an appointment. Do you remember Tic Verdun? Anakin went to meet him."

CHAPTER THIRTEEN

Anakin was starting to feel better. He had tried to tell himself that Soara had not been fair to him, but in truth, her words had shaken him. He had looked into her eyes and seen great disappointment there. He could tell himself that he would prove her wrong, but the loss of her respect was a blow. And what would she tell his Master?

He had worried about these things all the way to the meeting with Tic Verdun, but now they had shrunk to vague feelings at the back of his mind. He was too caught up in meeting Tic's friends and hearing what they had to say about Granta Omega. Already he had collected a number of facts about the elusive businessman. If he could manage to put the pieces together, he and Obi-Wan would have a place to start.

Tic's friends were all funny and smart. They had welcomed Anakin and seemed impressed at meeting "our first Jedi!" They poured him tea and sat around trying to prod their memories for facts about Granta Omega. They interrupted one another and corrected one another. But nobody interrupted Tic, Anakin noted. They all deferred to him, but in a way that Anakin could see was out of great respect.

Anakin was especially impressed with a young scientist named Mellora Falon. She had just graduated from an elite scientific institution even though she was only a few years older than Anakin. She had met Granta Omega on an expedition to the planet Uriek, and gave the most detailed account of him.

"He had a weakness for pastry," she said, smiling. "The really sweet, sticky kind. He ate an entire plate of sweesonberry rolls."

Tic Verdun shook his head. "Glad to see you noted the important things."

But everything was important. Anakin knew that. He could take that information back to Jocasta Nu and in about thirty seconds she could tell him every planet where the sweesonberries grew, and could give him a list of the best pastry makers in the Core Worlds.

"I just remembered something," Mellora said. "That morning, he said his favorite house was surrounded by sweesonberry bushes. He goes there for vacations. It's near the sea, too."

More information for Jocasta Nu. Anakin took another sip of the excellent tea Mellora had brewed. He felt warm and comfortable. Night had fallen, and the stars twinkled like hard points outside in the cold night. He thought about reaching for another piece of fruit, but he felt too lazy.

Just at the very moment he settled into his contentment, he felt a warning. There was a disturbance in the Force here. He realized that it had been there for some time. Anakin felt slow surprise trickle through him.

Here? But he was among friends. Perhaps he was confused. Perhaps he was wrong. Soara had showed him that his connection to the Force was not as clear as he'd once supposed.

He tried to focus on his feelings, but they seemed to run off his body like water. He blinked several times and realized he was sleepy. He had to struggle to stay awake. Mellora was speaking again, and he had to focus in order to hear her. Had his fight with Ferus tired him out so?

". . . more tea? No, I don't think you should." She laughed, her red lips parting. Her dark hair was as sleek as the pelt of a water animal.

"Anakin?" Tic's face seemed to loom in front of him. He patted Anakin's arm gently. "Are you all right? I have to tell you something. Are you listening?"

Anakin focused on Tic. "Yes?"

"Everything we told you about Granta Omega is a lie," Tic said, still smiling.

Anakin struggled to understand his meaning. "I . . . don't . . . understand."

"Oh, don't worry. You will."

"But we do have something to show you," Mellora said. "Something he owns." From beneath the folds of her white tunic she brought out a small pyramid. "Omega gave me this."

It was a Sith artifact. Now Anakin knew the origin of the disturbance he had detected. It grew stronger, and he felt nausea rise in his throat. He tried to sit up, but the chair now seemed to hold him down.

Mellora turned the cube in her hands. "At first I found the images disturbing. But Granta talked to me about them. Power can be disturbing. That's where its beauty lies. Do you understand?"

Anakin's tongue felt thick. "No." He had been so foolish. So incredibly foolish and naïve. He saw the mug on the table in front of him. He had drained every drop. He wasn't tired. He was drugged.

"Don't worry, we didn't poison you," Tic said. "It's because we have respect for the Jedi that we did this. We know it's the only way to slow you down."

Tic's voice had not changed. He still sounded friendly and warm. "We've immobilized you in order to talk to you. We don't wish to harm you."

"We only wish to discuss the Force," Mellora said.

The other faces turned to him. Now their bright interest, he saw, was not interest at all. It was not so simple. It was greed. They were ravenous for information about him. He had thought he was learning from them, but all the time, they were studying him.

"Mellora and I are the only scientists here," Tic said. "I'm afraid I lied to you about my friends. We are simply a group of ordinary beings who are interested in the extraordinary. We have a common interest in the Force."

"We wanted to find a Force-sensitive being to talk to about it," Mellora said.

In other words, Anakin thought, they were a Sith cult. No matter how friendly they seemed. No matter how much they wanted him to think they were harmless. He had tangled with a Sith cult before. Although they weren't Force-sensitive, they were drawn to the dark side and they could be dangerous.

But why Tic Verdun? He was a respected scientist.

And how do you know that? You don't know anything about him except that you liked him.

Anakin thought back to the mission on Haariden. He had liked Tic because Tic had seemed to understand him. He had been the bravest of the scientists, too. He had been the one to go off and scout for patrols. He had risked his life, they said . . .

He had been gone for hours, they said . . .

"Do you understand?" Tic asked him softly. "Do you, Anakin Skywalker?"

"You are Granta Omega," he said.

"Very good." Tic turned to the others, pleased. "You see how his mind continues to work? On an ordinary being, that drug would immobilize his thoughts as well as his legs."

Anakin thought about trying to rise. He thought he would have enough strength to reach the door. He had not begun to tap into the Force yet.

Wait. That's what Obi-Wan would say. He had enough strength for one try. He knew that. And if he had enough strength for only that, he had better plan it.

"Back on Haariden, you said the Force frustrates you," Tic said.

No. I spoke hastily. It was because of what happened with Darra. But Anakin said nothing. He did not want to have a conversation with Tic. Omega. He found it unnerving to see the same friendly look in his bright eyes, the good humor on his face.

"That interested me," Omega said. "I thought, this Jedi is different. He recognizes not only what power is, but what it isn't. What it can be. Power is . . . protection. It is what stands between you and losing what you have. I'm not talking about material things, either. I'm talking about . . . everything."

Anakin didn't understand. But then, he didn't want to.

Tic leaned forward. His warm eyes met Anakin's.

Not Tic. Granta Omega. He is not your friend.

The words Tic and Omega blurred in his mind. He remembered a man sitting on a snowy mountainside, his skin knitted together with synth-flesh. He could not reconcile the two images, the two men. It all seemed unreal.

"I've asked about you," Omega said. "I know you. I know you because I grew up like you. I wasn't a slave, but I might well have been. My mother worked at things she should not have, harder than she should have, longer than she should have — just for me."

My mother did the same.

"My mother worked herself to death for me," Omega said.

I can only hope that Shmi is well and safe.

"What is the Force for, if not to protect what you

have? Why should you give that up because you are a Jedi? The Force can bring you all the power you need. Yet the Jedi tell you that you must have nothing. Why is that?"

"Ours is a path of service," Anakin said.

"And who do you serve? The Senate?" Omega laughed softly. "A group of fools who can be bought?"

"We serve justice."

"Whose?"

"Justice does not have a master."

"Shouldn't it?" Omega leaned back again, resting against the pillows. "I am just a seeker, as you are. You have been told that the Sith belong to the dark side. Yet the Jedi know little of the Sith. What you don't know could fill galaxies. Well, you do know one thing — that there is one Sith still alive. I know this, too. I wanted to be rich enough to find that Sith. Then one day I realized that was wrong. The only way I would find a Sith is if I was rich enough, powerful enough, so that he wanted to find *me*. I am not rich enough yet. But I will be."

Omega paused. "I'm not Force-sensitive. I can never be a Sith. I have found something at last that I cannot buy. But I can be close to that power. I can sit at his side, as I am sitting by your side."

"That's why you attack the Jedi," Anakin said. "You want to impress him."

"Yes, you see? It's nothing personal." Omega leaned closer to him. "Don't you think I could have killed you if I wanted?"

"No," Anakin said. "I know you *think* you could have."

"I like you," Omega said. "I liked what I saw on Haariden. Your Master you can keep. Typical Jedi." He waved a hand. "But you . . . you I like."

"I'm honored," Anakin said.

"Sarcasm from a Jedi? I knew I liked you." Omega leaned back against the cushions and crossed an ankle over his leg comfortably. "You're different because you didn't grow up in that Temple. You know how power works because you were ground down beneath it. You know how the powerless have only their dignity to comfort them, and how, some days, that is not enough. Not nearly enough."

Shmi. He had left her with nothing but her dignity.

Mellora stood restlessly. "Let me show him."

"No."

"Yes." Mellora reached into her pocket and withdrew Darra's lightsaber. "I've been learning how to use it. One day I will fight a Jedi."

The Force he had kept at bay shot through him, revitalizing his muscles. The sight of Darra's lightsaber in Mellora's hand had done it. He felt strength move through him. He knew he could rise now.

Even Omega looked amazed when he shot to his feet. He activated his lightsaber in a motion so fast they could not follow it with their eyes.

"How about today?" he taunted, taking a step toward her. "Are you ready to fight a Jedi today?" His voice was thick and it was an effort to get the words out. He could feel his leg muscles trembling but he knew they couldn't see it.

"Well, well," Omega breathed. "Impressive."

But the others were not so calm. They drew blasters.

"Shoot him!" Mellora shrilled. She activated the lightsaber clumsily.

Anakin took a step. He felt unsteady but in control. Mellora began to wave the lightsaber. She tried to execute an offensive thrust, but the lightsaber swung crazily. She was not able to balance it.

"Mellora, don't be foolish," Omega warned.

But Mellora did not drop the lightsaber, and Anakin was more afraid that she would injure herself than he was of the blasters. He knew his usual control would be off, so he would have to compensate. He could not risk a complicated move. Simple was best.

Keeping the lightsaber in one hand, he struck out with a strong kick in order to dislodge Darra's lightsaber from her hand. But Mellora surprised him by twirling away. She was still hampered by the lightsaber, but the combination of Anakin's slowed reaction time and her own skill caused him to miss. Anakin stumbled, and to his surprise he could not recover easily.

He went down on one hand. Mellora smiled. She raised the lightsaber. Even she could probably manage a downward stroke.

He called on the Force. It surged through him. He balanced on one hand and swept his feet in an arc that hit Mellora on the ankles and took her down. Darra's lightsaber went flying.

The others scattered, afraid of the lightsaber, and wildly fired their blasters. Granta Omega looked up, his mouth open, his hands outstretched for the lightsaber.

Desperately, Anakin threw himself at Granta Omega. He hit him broadside, and they both fell. The lightsaber clattered to the floor, deactivated.

The group saw Anakin on the floor with their leader and pointed their blasters at him. He raised his own lightsaber to deflect the fire, but he could see that he would not be able to hold out for long.

Then suddenly a blue blur appeared through the door. Metal peeled back and Obi-Wan leaped through the opening.

CHAPTER FOURTEEN

For a moment, no one moved. Anakin felt as though he had used up his last reserve of strength. He was sprawled on the floor, looking up at his Master. Mellora lay frozen, her eyes moving from the lightsaber on the floor to the activated one in Obi-Wan's hand.

Granta Omega laughed at the same moment that the blasters fired.

Obi-Wan stepped forward, his lightsaber constantly moving, deflecting the fire. Blaster bolts pinged off the walls. Obi-Wan came and stood over Anakin, who began to try to rise.

Granta Omega's fingers closed over the fallen lightsaber's hilt. With the other hand, he reached down and activated a switch on a device hanging on his belt. A door in a console opened and released five seekers into the air. They honed in on Obi-Wan and peppered him with blaster fire. Obi-Wan swung his lightsaber, deflecting the fire, and leaped in the air to slash the seekers one by one. He had his hands full. Anakin watched as Granta Omega, Mellora, and the rest of the group escaped through a window. Omega held Darra's lightsaber.

Anakin saw it happening and felt responsible again. If his Master hadn't needed to protect him, he would have captured them all. A last surge of strength helped him down one seeker with an awkward swing from the floor. Obi-Wan took out the last two.

He reached down and helped Anakin to his feet. "What happened?"

"They drugged me. The mug . . ."

Obi-Wan picked up the mug and shoved it in his tunic. "We'll analyze it at the Temple."

"They had a Sith artifact. A Holocron pyramid. Tic is Granta Omega —"

"I know." Obi-Wan searched the room. "They must have taken it with them." He crouched in front of the console. He reached in and rummaged through a travel kit. He threw aside several basic items, then held up a portable scanner. He studied it for a moment. "Now this is interesting."

Anakin nodded. He felt as though it took him several long minutes to complete the nod. Obi-Wan noted this and jumped to his feet.

"We'd better get you back to the Temple."

Obi-Wan stood in front of the assembled Jedi Council. In one hand he held the portable scanner. He stood respectfully as the Jedi Council sat, absorbing what he had told them.

"Certain you are of this," Yoda said.

"Completely."

"Ambitious, this Granta Omega is."

"That is the danger. He infiltrated the Senate expedition because he knew it was going to examine the mineral rights of Haariden. It was the Senate's secret plan to defuse the civil war. I read the expedition's report. It was incomplete, but it shows one thing clearly — there is an active volcano on Haariden. The mountain Kaachtari will soon have a massive eruption, an eruption so powerful it will change the coastline nearby. The titanite that has been hidden in the planet's core will spew out with the lava. A giant tidal wave will form and cover the landmass. Sano Sauro has buried the report, but it is in the Senate archives." Obi-Wan held up the portable scanner. "This is an underwater scanner. He is planning to mine the titanite from the sea. He will be able to do so if we don't stop him. I believe he wants to control the bacta market for the entire galaxy."

"What do you wish to do, Master Kenobi?" Ki-Adi-Mundi asked. "He has not committed a crime."

"Not for the bacta, no, not yet," Obi-Wan said. "Although he did use an alias to get on a Senate expedition, and that would lead to censure, at least. He has committed serious crimes against the Jedi, however. He has paid bounty hunters and soldiers to attack us on two occasions. He drugged my Padawan."

"This is something you know, but you must also prove," Ki-Adi-Mundi said. His second heart pulsed in his high skull. "That is the difficulty."

"I can bring him back to Coruscant for questioning by the Senate," Obi-Wan said. "At least we can prevent what he plans. He wants to gain even greater power and wealth in order to attract the hidden Sith Lord. He admitted this to Anakin."

"Perhaps he would attract him," Mace Windu said. "If we let him, if we stood back and watched, we would be able to track the Sith Lord ourselves. He would be flushed out of hiding before he is ready."

"Are you saying we should not stop Omega?" Obi-Wan asked in disbelief.

Mace Windu looked at him sharply. "We are not drawing conclusions. We are speculating."

"All sides of the issue we must examine," Yoda said.

Mace Windu swiveled in his chair to look out over the twinkling lights of Coruscant. "Darkness lies ahead. We can all feel it. Is this a place where we can turn? Where we can flush out our enemy and expose him?"

"But if we don't go after Omega, he will control the market on bacta," Obi-Wan said. "He could do anything. Raise the price too high. Create shortages. I have no doubt he would do these things. Millions would suffer."

"More millions suffer in our visions of the future," Mace said. He was still looking out at the lights. He seemed to be speaking to himself. "We see much pain."

"Visions can only show us what *may* be," Obi-Wan said. "Granta Omega can do great harm now."

A buzz of conversation began among the Council Members. Mace Windu consulted with Yoda. Adi Gallia leaned over to speak with Even Piell. It was highly unusual for the Council to break into private consultations. The gravity of the issue caused it. There were too many important questions connected with it.

"Go, Obi-Wan must." Yaddle's soft voice stopped the Council Members. Everyone turned to her with great courtesy. Yaddle rarely spoke, but when she did, she always seemed to sum up the conclusions they would have reached eventually.

She blinked her light gray-blue eyes, which were so like Yoda's. "Suffering we cannot allow in order to prevent what we fear. Stop it we must when we can."

Yoda leaned forward on his gimer stick. "Correct, Yaddle is. Has your Padawan recovered, Obi-Wan?"

Obi-Wan nodded. "I have arranged transport. I can be on Haariden by sunrise."

"Dangerous it is," Yoda said. "Soon, the eruption will occur. Take chances you must not."

"May the Force be with you," Mace Windu said, concluding the meeting. He still looked troubled.

Obi-Wan bowed. He left the Council chamber and hurried directly to the med clinic. Every moment counted.

Anakin was sitting up on the med couch, swinging his legs. He was pale, but he looked up at Obi-Wan expectantly.

"I hear you are cleared for duty," Obi-Wan said. "Are you sure you are fully recovered?"

Anakin nodded. "Yes. Where are we going?"

"Back to Haariden," Obi-Wan said. "We're going to watch a volcano erupt."

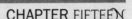

CHAPTER FIFTEEN

As the Galan starfighter shot through hyperspace, Anakin had some time to rest and think.

The rest he needed. He did not want to tell Obi-Wan that even though the drug had worn off, his senses still felt blurred, as if there were a veil between him and everything else. But he knew the veil would lift. He could feel clarity returning with every passing minute.

What he did not know was how to sort out his feelings about Granta Omega. He was not naïve enough to think that evil announced itself by knocking on one's door with an iron fist. But he had not expected evil to come cloaked in quite so much charm.

He had enjoyed the earlier time he'd spent with Granta Omega. When he'd known him as Tic Verdun, he had laughed at the things he said and felt warmed by his friendship. They had not known each other long, but Anakin had to admit it: He'd felt kinship with Tic. On Haariden, he had offered him friendship. He had made him feel a little less alone.

How could he reconcile his feelings with the knowledge that Omega's one desire was to worship at the heart of evil? An evil that had murdered the one being who had saved Anakin from a life of slavery: Qui-Gon Jinn.

Obi-Wan had been in the small ship's library, checking the geological reports on Haariden. He came to sit by Anakin. "Not too much longer. Is there something you want to discuss with me, Padawan?"

He wasn't ready to talk about it. "No," Anakin said.

Obi-Wan hesitated. "Before I arrived, did you talk much to the others?"

Anakin nodded. "They fed me false information about Granta Omega. They were making things up to tease me even as he sat right in front of me. I see that now. I feel foolish."

"It is not something to feel foolish about. Those who set out to deceive are the true fools." Obi-Wan paused. "And Omega himself? What did you think of him?"

The gentleness in his Master's tone undid Anakin's reserve. "I *liked* him," he burst out. "How could I like such a being?"

"I would guess that is because he is likable," Obi-Wan said dryly.

His Master's calmness made Anakin feel better. "Shouldn't the Force have alerted me to the dark side in him?"

"Not necessarily," Obi-Wan said. "The Force is not a truth-detector. We can rely on it, but we can't expect it to save us. We must save ourselves. We must use our own intuition, our own intelligence. Your feelings about Granta Omega don't have anything to do with the Force. They have everything to do with experience."

"Meaning I don't have enough?"

"Maybe," Obi-Wan said. "Perhaps I wouldn't have picked up on Omega's true character, either. But I have seen enough to know that evil can wear a charming face, my young Padawan. Charisma is not a virtue. It's a trait. It is not good or bad. Evil people can possess it. They often do and it is what makes them dangerous."

"He says he is a seeker, just as the Jedi are," Anakin said. "He says the Jedi fear the Sith, but they know nothing of them."

"He is wrong," Obi-Wan said. "The Jedi have deep knowledge of the Sith. Have you forgotten that one of them killed Qui-Gon?"

"That knowledge is with me every day," Anakin said

quietly. "But it is also part of the problem. When I think of evil, I see that Sith Lord's face. I do not see Granta Omega's."

"Evil has many faces," Obi-Wan responded. "It can masquerade as vision. One must look beneath the words, beneath the mask."

An indicator light flashed. Obi-Wan sprang to his feet. "We've arrived."

Obi-Wan slid into the pilot's seat. Anakin sat next to him. The starfighter shuddered slightly as they came out of hyperspace. The planet of Haariden lay ahead.

Obi-Wan entered the coordinates for landing. He shot Anakin a quick questioning look. "Are you ready to face him again?"

He was not sure, but he knew he had to be. "I am ready, Master."

He felt the dark side of the Force gather as they entered the planet's atmosphere. As they drew closer they could see the large areas of land that had been laid to waste by war.

"I am not happy to see this place again," Obi-Wan murmured.

The craft skimmed over the foothills. Obi-Wan landed in a valley near an outcropping of trees.

"We need to keep clear of the eruption site," he said. "We'll track Omega on swoop bikes. According to

Jocasta Nu, we have about an hour before the volcano begins to erupt."

"Not much time," Anakin said as they hurried toward the stowed swoops.

"It will have to be enough."

Anakin swung his leg over the swoop. He was feeling better, but heaviness still seemed to hang on him, clouding his mind. The med staff had assured him that the drug was completely out of his system. He was not sure why he wasn't feeling himself yet. He suspected it had something to do with the dark feeling of doom he received from this planet.

They took off on their swoops, gliding over the hills and heading for the rugged mountains ahead. One mountain pushed high above the rest, seeming to thrust itself out of the planet's core. It was topped with snow, its peak hidden in the clouds.

"That's it," Obi-Wan said. "That's Kaachtari."

They pushed the swoops to maximum speed. The air turned colder as they rose to higher elevations. Suddenly, Anakin saw a column of steam spurt from the ground below. He swerved the swoop just in time to avoid being scalded.

"We're in the danger zone now," Obi-Wan said. "Be careful."

As they rode on, Anakin saw that deep fissures had

cracked the earth and split gigantic boulders in two. The steam rose hundreds of meters high in some places. He heard a muffled sound, like a faraway starfighter engine roaring.

"Groundquakes," Obi-Wan said. "Small ones, so far."

Anakin looked ahead. He saw a line of soldiers hiking down the mountain. He pointed them out to Obi-Wan.

His Master frowned. "This area was supposed to have been evacuated. Let's get a little closer."

They descended. Hearing the noise, the soldiers looked up. Some of them raised blasters.

"Master?"

"Don't worry." Obi-Wan suddenly zoomed down, landing directly in front of them. Anakin followed his Master to the head of the line to stand before a gaunt soldier with a grimy face and a beard gray with ash.

"I see we meet again, Captain Welflet," Obi-Wan said.

The captain nodded a greeting. "I thought you evacuated." A groundquake shook the area, and the captain staggered. "You should have."

"We did. We came back. We're looking for Granta Omega," Obi-Wan said. "Have you seen him?"

"No," the captain said. "I have enough worries."

He stared at Obi-Wan when he said this, but Anakin knew he was lying.

"This area was evacuated," Obi-Wan said. "The volcano is about to erupt."

"I know," Captain Welflet said. "But we had word of enemy patrols in the area. They are using the eruption to gain land."

"But you will all die," Obi-Wan said. "The eruption will cover all this." He swung an arm out. "The scientists know this. The sensors indicate it."

Captain Welflet snorted. "Scientists and sensors. This is our land. We are not going to lose it."

"I see you have some new weaponry since I saw you last," Obi-Wan remarked.

The captain shifted his gaze. "Is the Jedi so interested in our weaponry?"

The mountain rumbled. A steam column suddenly split the rocky ground and spewed into the air.

"We don't have much time," Obi-Wan said. "Let me tell you what I think, and what you don't know. I think you accepted payment in weapons for land that will be useless to you. But you were tricked."

"That is an interesting supposition," the captain said cautiously.

"Granta Omega paid you for the rights to the new sea," Obi-Wan said. "What you don't know is that he wants it for a reason. The volcano will deposit titanite on the land before the wave brings the water. He will mine it and make a fortune. And you will lose out."

"He said he wanted it for a fish farm," the captain muttered. "And we believed him! He had us meet him here to do the deal." He looked down at the plains below. "It belongs to him now."

"Tell me where he is, and I might be able to help you," Obi-Wan said.

"He does not deserve our loyalty," the captain said. "He is above, on the ridge, conducting experiments. Here are the coordinates." The captain gave them to Obi-Wan.

"You must get down the mountain as quickly as you can," Obi-Wan said.

"We have air transport below. But we are on the lookout for the enemy."

"Forget the enemy," Obi-Wan said. "If you don't, you will die."

"Then we will die," Captain Welflet said. "But we will die on our land."

Obi-Wan swung his leg back over the swoop and motioned to Anakin. He plugged the coordinates into the onboard computer.

"We must hurry, Padawan," he said. "I don't like the look of this scanner. The groundquakes are intensifying."

"But the captain and his men," Anakin said. "How can we leave them?"

Obi-Wan shook his head sadly. "I cannot change his mind, Padawan. They must do what they will do, and we must do the same."

They took off to the spot where the captain had left Granta Omega. Flying was difficult now, as the steam hissed suddenly into the air, sometimes followed by showers of large rocks. Anakin felt dread rising within him. He did not want to see Granta Omega again. Yet he had to.

They saw him high on a snowy ridge. He was with Mellora. They were both dressed in white thermal gear to protect them from the cold. They were packing up their equipment and heading for their swoops. They clearly did not trust anyone else to pinpoint the titanite before the eruption.

Obi-Wan leaned over his swoop, urging the machine to go faster. Granta Omega looked up and saw them. Even from that distance, Anakin could tell he was dismayed. He spoke a quick word to Mellora and they took off.

"We'll follow them to the ship," Obi-Wan said. "We can commandeer it and return them to Coruscant."

"It can't be that easy," Anakin said.

"It won't be," Obi-Wan said.

Granta and Mellora did not attempt to lose the Jedi. No doubt they knew they could not. The Jedi gained on them, but Mellora and Omega managed to reach their SoroSuub at the foot of the volcano. Omega activated the landing ramp and they flew inside.

"We can make it!" Obi-Wan shouted as the landing ramp began to close.

Anakin zoomed alongside his Master. They angled their swoops as the ramp slid closed. They slid inside, feeling the whoosh of air as the ramp slid into place.

The cockpit of the ship was empty.

Obi-Wan leaped off the swoop and activated his lightsaber in one motion. He ran through the SoroSuub. It took only a few seconds to discover what had happened.

"They flew out the cargo door as we came in through the landing ramp," Obi-Wan said, disgusted. "He planned it."

He ran to the cockpit controls. He stabbed at the activation key for the landing ramp, then the cargo doors.

"He's locked them." He tried the engines. Nothing happened. "The ship is in complete lockdown."

Obi-Wan's face was dark with anger. Anakin watched, fascinated, as his Master absorbed his anger and then released it.

"So here we are," Obi-Wan said in a measured tone. "Locked in." He crossed to the cockpit windscreen. Granta Omega and Mellora were nowhere in sight. But the mountain was. It filled their vision as it belched rocks and steam.

As they watched, the ship suddenly shook with the tremor of a huge groundquake. The scene in front of them vibrated. Anakin couldn't believe what he was seeing. The peak was now disintegrating. Huge chunks of the mountain were falling away. The entire side of the volcano was collapsing in a tremendous landside.

And they were in its path.

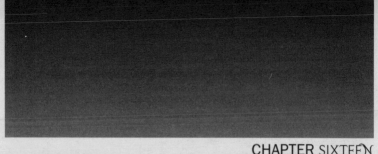

CHAPTER SIXTEEN

Obi-Wan tried the engines again. "I don't know how to override this."

"Let me try." There was nothing Anakin couldn't do with engines. He slid open the panel to the engine and slithered inside. "This will take me about twenty minutes."

"We don't have twenty," Obi-Wan said. He had already calculated the speed of the landslide. "We have maybe five before the lava pours out. If we're lucky. We'll have to cut our way out."

Anakin scrambled out and followed Obi-Wan to the opening to the ramp. Obi-Wan began to try to cut the durasteel away.

"Something's wrong," he muttered as Anakin joined him. "The ship's hull should be thin here. We should be able to cut through in minutes."

"It's going to take us longer than that," Anakin said.

The minutes ticked by as they worked at the metal. Obi-Wan looked out the windscreen to check the progress of the eruption. The noise was now like the roar of a fleet of engines. "We're not going to make it."

They looked at each other. They hadn't given up hope. There was a way out. There always was.

They just didn't have much time to figure it out.

Lava was now spewing out of the top of the mountain. Whole kilometers of dirt and rocks mixed with hot lava would soon be barreling down the steep slope.

Obi-Wan pushed his lightsaber through the door. He began to move it downward, straining with the effort. Anakin joined him, the sweat rolling down his face.

Suddenly and violently, molten lava poured out of the volcano at frightening speed. The avalanche of rock and lava smashed against the ship. The jolt threw them across the cockpit and slammed them against the opposite wall. The craft tilted onto one side, sending them crashing onto the floor. The ship jolted downhill at incredible speed, carried by the force of the landslide.

Anakin hung on to the wall. Looking straight up, he could see through the cockpit windscreen. All he saw was rocks and lava obscuring his view of the sky. He knew where they were being carried. The rock slide would drop them into the sea. They would sink. Or else they would be caught in the giant tidal wave that was forming even now.

His head slammed against the side of the ship. He held on as his teeth rattled. Death was near. Anakin could feel it. Now he understood why he had felt so uneasy on this planet. Here death had waited for him.

Obi-Wan suddenly pounded against the ship's wall with his lightsaber hilt as they bounced down the mountain, swept along by the lava flow. Anakin had never seen his Master give way to his anger before.

"That's it," Obi-Wan shouted over the awful roaring noise. "It's a ship within a ship. That's why the walls are so thick. Anakin, help me find it."

"Find what?" he shouted.

"The cockpit. The real cockpit!" Obi-Wan scrambled along the wall, knocking on it with the hilt of his lightsaber. "Listen for something hollow."

The lurching of the ship made it hard to maneuver, but Anakin followed his Master. He knocked against the wall with his lightsaber hilt.

"Here!" Obi-Wan shouted suddenly. He activated his lightsaber and began to cut through the wall.

Anakin grabbed handholds and fought his way toward his Master. He worked alongside him. Obi-Wan was right. The metal was thinner here. It peeled back in strips. They were being pounded by the landslide and it was hard to cut, but they struggled to finish.

At last there was an opening large enough to crawl inside. To Anakin's surprise, he found a complete cockpit with engine controls.

"Can you fly it?" Obi-Wan asked.

Anakin nodded. He strapped himself into the seat. The ship was on its side. He pushed the left engine and the ship rose straight up.

He kept pushing the engine and the ship revolved. Then he accelerated, and they shot through the lava and the pummeling rocks into the clear air above.

Obi-Wan sank back into the seat next to him. "That was close," he panted.

"I wouldn't want it any closer," Anakin admitted. "Where to, Master?"

"They'll be watching from a safe distance," Obi-Wan said. "Along the coast, but out of range of the wave." He bent over the scanner, comparing its readings to the map on the shipboard computer. "Let's try these coordinates." He pointed them out to Anakin.

He nodded and piloted the ship back toward the eruption. He would skirt the worst of it, but they would have a bumpy flight. Rocks hammered down on the shell of the ship, and the air pockets were deep. The ship kept slamming into them.

"Master, look!" Anakin pointed ahead. The Haariden captain and the soldiers were trapped on the plain as the landslide headed toward them. They had turned to face it. There was nowhere to run.

"See if we can make it!" Obi-Wan ordered. "Push the engines!"

Anakin accelerated till the engines screamed, piloting the ship straight into the spew of lava and rocks. The ship shook as a boulder struck it. Then another.

Captain Welflet saw them approaching and lifted a hand. Anakin did not know if it was in thanks or farewell. In the next instant the landslide had swept him and his soldiers to their deaths. They were buried under the land they had fought over so desperately.

Shaken, Anakin pushed the engines to rise above the eruption again. He felt a sickness in his stomach.

His Master said nothing, but closed his eyes for a moment.

"I wish I hadn't seen that," Anakin said.

Obi-Wan opened his eyes. "Such is the life of a Jedi."

The cockpit indicators began to swing wildly. The ship lurched to one side.

"I think the power cells were hit," Anakin said. "We've got to land. The power is draining fast."

"We're almost out of range of the eruption," Obi-Wan said, his eyes on the monitor. "Keep going . . ."

Anakin held onto the controls as the ship lurched again. He heard the whine of the power cells as they powered down. "Master, I'm losing the ship."

"All right. Land it where you can."

Anakin found a smooth area of sand. They were near the coast of the sea here. He set the ship down bumpily. He had just enough energy to land.

The ship settled into the sand and the engines cut out.

"Good thing we still have the swoops," Obi-Wan said.

They climbed out of the concealed cockpit. The swoop bikes were smashed from the rough journey, but still functioned. Anakin activated the landing ramp from the interior cockpit. It squealed as the metal rubbed against metal, but it opened far enough for them to slide out with the swoops.

The air was thick with ash. A strange smell was in the air. It was like burning, but it wasn't born of flame or smoke.

"It is the core," Obi-Wan said. "Metals and molten rock."

They piloted the swoops away from the ship and began to search for Omega and Mellora. At last they came upon them on a plateau that overlooked the sea. There they would be protected from the tidal wave.

Granta Omega saw them coming. There was no way to surprise them. Anakin saw him bend down. He settled something against his shoulder. A missile launcher.

"Master —"

"I see it. Dive, Padawan."

They dived as the first missile headed their way. Its target was Obi-Wan. His Master leaned to one side and the missile missed him by a meter.

Another missile was launched. Anakin dived, but the missile was targeted at Obi-Wan again. His Master practiced evasive action, and this time, the missile missed him by mere centimeters.

Another missile was launched. This one, too, was headed for Obi-Wan.

"He's only aiming at me," Obi-Wan called. "Get closer, Anakin!"

Anakin zoomed past the missile. He saw Omega smile and target a slowing Obi-Wan again, but Mellora had vanished. He pushed the swoop engines past maximum.

He jumped the last few meters just as Omega launched another missile. Anakin glanced back in time to see his Master barely evade it. His swoop seemed damaged by the action.

Omega had anticipated Anakin. He held the missile launcher against his shoulder, his finger hovering over the activation button. "Your Master's swoop is over-heating. He doesn't have good maneuverability any-more. This one might get him. I've always thought that to be personally responsible for the death of a Jedi would truly help me make my mark. Would you really miss him so much, Anakin?" He grinned at Anakin, the ash-filled wind whipping his dark hair across his face.

"Don't," Anakin said. "You will regret it."

"I knew you'd get out of that ship!" Omega cried. "You will make a great Jedi Knight one day, Anakin Sky-walker. But you will be even greater if you listen to me!"

Anakin took a step toward him. "My Master and I re-quest that you return to Coruscant with us for ques-tioning by the authorities."

Omega sighed. "What a kind invitation. I'm afraid I'll have to refuse. I'm busy, you see." He inched backward toward his swoop, his finger still hovering over the launch button.

Anakin leaped feet first. But instead of going for Omega, he kicked the swoop. Omega's eyes widened in shock as the swoop was knocked over the edge of the plateau. At the same time, Anakin's arm flew out and came down on the missile launcher, dislodging it from Omega's shoulder. With dismay, Anakin saw that the readied missile was launched as the launcher hit the ground.

Omega fumbled inside his tunic. Anakin heard the whine of a swoop engine behind him. He whirled in time to sidestep Mellora, who headed toward them at top speed. Omega tossed a thermal detonator as he clumsily leaped aboard Mellora's swoop.

Anakin caught the detonator and tossed it as far as he could. The explosion sent shock waves through the air. He raced back to his own swoop and leaped aboard.

Omega released seeker droids into the air. There were at least ten, heading toward Obi-Wan like a flock of deadly attack birds. Obi-Wan now had to contend with the droids and the tracking missile.

Anakin swung at the droids with his lightsaber as his swoop lurched crazily. He was trying to corner Omega and Mellora against the sheer face of the ridge, but the two zoomed below him, heading for the sandy plain.

It was a tactical error. Now they were heading toward the sea.

Obi-Wan turned his swoop at the last possible moment and the missile impacted on a seeker droid. He joined Anakin. They zoomed after Mellora and Omega.

The seekers were as thick in the air as the ash. Obi-Wan and Anakin swung their lightsabers constantly, sending them smashing down to the ground below.

Obi-Wan's speeder engine was smoking badly. "I'm overheating," he called to Anakin. "Some shrapnel pierced the engine."

Anakin maneuvered his swoop close to his Master. "Hop aboard."

Obi-Wan balanced on the seat and leaped onto Anakin's swoop. The swoop rocked from side to side, but Anakin straightened it and kept on flying. Obi-Wan stood on the seat behind him, balancing easily. His lightsaber was a blur as he swung it at the attack droids.

"Master, the water!" Anakin called.

Far out on the sea, they could see a wave. It was as tall as a Coruscant skyscraper. It was a wall of water moving at more than a hundred kilometers an hour.

Omega and Mellora had gone too far in order to escape. Now they were trapped between the oncoming wave and the Jedi. They hovered in the air, staring at the wave. Omega looked back at the approaching Jedi defiantly. Mellora only looked afraid.

Anakin pulled up the swoop close to Omega. They could hear the eerie sound of the wave now, a sound like no other Anakin had ever heard.

"You must come with us now," Obi-Wan said, his lightsaber raised.

"Granta, it's over," Mellora said, her eyes on the approaching wave. "We must —"

In answer, Omega wrenched the controls from Mellora. He shot the swoop straight toward the wall of water. They could see Mellora's mouth forming a scream before its sound was snatched away by the roar of the titanic wave.

Grimly, Anakin headed after them. He stayed below Omega's swoop, hoping to force them upward. He didn't know if they would be able to clear the wave in time.

Omega swerved up, trying to clear the wave. Mellora had Darra's lightsaber and was trying to activate it. Anakin didn't know why. There was little she could do with it. Perhaps she wanted to force Omega to surrender.

Omega suddenly reached out and casually put his foot against Mellora. With a push, he shoved her off the swoop.

She fell toward the wave, shrieking.

Anakin gunned the motor and dove under her. Obi-Wan caught her in his arms. The lightsaber fell from her fingers, and Anakin lurched to the side in order to snatch it from the air. Then he zoomed above as the water curled over their heads.

They couldn't make it. He took a deep breath as they went straight into the top of the wave. He felt the power of the water drive them backward. The controls shook in his hand. He heard the engine whine. He could only see water, and he was confused now. Were they heading up or down?

Then the Force entered him, and he did not see the water as a wall. He saw it for what it was. Full of particles, full of gaps, honeycombed with light. He headed for the gaps, willing the swoop engine to obey him.

They broke through the water into the air. Mellora clung to Obi-Wan, gasping.

Omega was a speck in the distance, heading away from them.

"He would have killed me!" Mellora choked.

Anakin hovered in the air, watching the speck disappear. They had lost him again.

"Head for our ship, Padawan," Obi-Wan said.

Anakin turned back toward safety. He did not believe that Omega wanted to kill Mellora. He had pushed her off knowing that the Jedi would save her. He just wanted to get away.

But it was better that Mellora not know that.

"I know where he is going," she told the Jedi. "I know where he goes when he loses. I can take you there."

"You don't have to," Obi-Wan said. "I know where he is going, too."

CHAPTER SEVENTEEN

Because of the eruption, hostilities had ceased temporarily on Haariden. They left Mellora with the authorities there with instructions to hold her until the Senate could send a ship for her. But they could not be certain how long she would be held. It was clear that she was prepared to lie her way out of trouble.

"She hates him now," Obi-Wan said as they hurried to their ship. "I only hope she sees what he really is. He would sacrifice her young life to save his own."

"But he knew we would catch her," Anakin said.

Obi-Wan shot his Padawan a curious look. "Are you certain of that?"

Anakin said nothing. Disquiet settled inside Obi-Wan as they both jumped into their craft. He plugged in the coordinates for Nierport Seven. They were so close behind Granta Omega. They just might catch him.

"How do you know where he is going, Master?" Anakin asked as they shot into hyperspace.

"It was the ship within a ship that told me," Obi-Wan explained. "I remembered his boyhood home. The walls were thicker than the other houses, but not too thick that they didn't blend in. But when I thought about it, I realized that the proportions were slightly off. I think there is a hidden room there. A room in the walls themselves."

Dusk was settling on Nierport Seven when they arrived. They landed on the outskirts of the settlement and hurried to the house.

There were no lights inside. Obi-Wan took out his lightsaber and cut a hole in the door.

The house was empty. Even the bedroll and stove were gone.

"We are too late," Anakin said.

"Yes," Obi-Wan said. "He must have assumed that Mellora would tell us what she knew."

He felt along the walls, knocking them with his lightsaber hilt. When he found what he was looking for, he cut through the walls with his lightsaber. Here the stone was only centimeters thick, bound to durasteel walls.

Beyond the wall was a room filled with datascreens. Obi-Wan and Anakin climbed through the hole.

Obi-Wan began to access the files. One after another he called up the holofiles. They were coded, but he was confident that the Jedi could crack them. He would take them back to the Temple.

"These must be his companies," he said. "His aliases are here, text docs, his other homes, bases of operations . . . it's all here. We've got him. All his secrets are now ours."

"It looks like he has an entire fleet of starships on some planet in the Outer Rim," Anakin said. "The planet's name is coded."

As he read the file, the letters began to fade. "Master —"

"The files are disappearing," Obi-Wan said. He quickly hit the keys, tapping furiously. "I can't stop it."

They watched as the information disappeared into fragments of light. The light dissolved into particles.

"He instituted a wipe from wherever he is," Obi-Wan said. "Now it is as though he never existed. He truly is a void."

They stared at the empty air. It was as if Granta Omega were mocking them from wherever he was.

"Now he has no past," Anakin said.

"And he's just become more dangerous than ever," Obi-Wan said. "He has nothing to lose."

Obi-Wan watched the emotion flit over his Padawan's face. Confusion was there, and wonderment. Granta Omega had touched something in Anakin that Obi-Wan could only guess at. Perhaps it was their similar origins, the desolation of the places they'd known as children. Perhaps it was the way they had left their pasts behind. Perhaps it was simply that for the first time, Anakin had seen evil coupled with charisma, and was struggling to understand it.

He wasn't sure what it was. But it worried him.

Yes, the Jedi had a dangerous enemy. It wasn't Omega's cleverness that concerned Obi-Wan. It wasn't his desire to impress a Sith Lord he had never met. It was the strange pull he had for his Padawan. Granta Omega might turn out to be the most dangerous enemy they would ever have to face.